A BEAUMONT FAMILY
CHRISTMAS

THE BEAUMONT SERIES

A BEAUMONT FAMILY CHRISTMAS
THE BEAUMONT SERIES

Copyright © 2020
Heidi McLaughlin

COVER DESIGN: Okay Creations
EDITING: Briggs Consulting

❀ Created with Vellum

1

JENNA

My phone rings, pulling me away from the novel I picked up the other day at the secondhand bookstore. I set it down and glance at the screen, expecting it to be Jimmy or Eden, but I am pleasantly surprised to see two tiny pictures staring back at me. Pressing the answer button, I pick my phone up and bring it eye level. The grin on my face is cheek to cheek as I stare at my two best friends. I love technology.

"Okay," Josie says, without saying hi. She's a right to the point type of person, which I enjoy. No beating around the bush from her. "Here's the deal. I rented this massive house for Christmas in Stowe, Vermont, and I want us all to be together. I know I'm demanding a lot here, especially since we're all so spread out, but I thought it would be nice if we could spend the holiday together."

Katelyn's eyes go wide, and I'm instantly curious what she's thinking. On the other hand, Josie is sitting as close to her phone as she can, probably trying to decipher what Katelyn and I are thinking.

What am I thinking?

"I love this idea," I say excitedly.

"We're in," Katelyn adds.

Josie dances around as best she can while holding her phone. "You have no idea how thrilled I am. Liam will be happy too. I think he misses Harrison and Jimmy but won't say anything."

"I don't know why you don't just move to California," I say. At first, when Jimmy proposed we move, I was hesitant. I love Beaumont, and Josie is there. I couldn't imagine being anywhere else or leaving her after she had done so much for me. But after spending time in Los Angeles and being on the beach, I knew I could easily live here. It was the sun and access to the beach that sold me. Plus, Jimmy wanted to be here. Even though he's not extremely close to his dad, he wanted to be around him. They have an odd relationship, and it's very strained, mostly because James refuses to be a part of his youngest child's life. Chelsea finally gave up harassing us on James's whereabouts once the court ordered him to pay child support. It was about this time that James reached out to Jimmy, groveling for forgiveness. Forgive, but never forget, is how Jimmy approaches his father, which is more than I would be able to do. Despite all of this, James is a good grandfather to Eden, and that's all that matters to me.

Josie sighs. "I don't know. I've thought about it. I know Liam would be happier there, but Beaumont is home. I have the shop, and Paige is still in school."

"And there is no way she'd let you take her away from Mack," Katelyn interjects.

Katelyn and I laugh, and Josie's eyes go wide. She looks over her shoulder before coming closer to the camera. "Liam is going to kill that boy, I swear. Or I might kill Nick for moving back to Beaumont to begin with."

"What's going on?" I ask.

"Just teenage drama. One week they like each other, the next week they're dating. And then the next week, Paige never wants to speak to him as long as she lives. Rinse and repeat."

"Sounds like Eden," I tell them. "Every other month it's a new surfer or a guy from her school. I can't keep track. She's such a heartbreaker. Secretly, though, I'm happy she's not in a committed relationship. I want her to focus on school."

"I'm sure Jimmy is more than happy," Katelyn adds.

"You have no idea. Okay, enough about the teens, tell us about this fabulous house you've rented, Josie!"

"It's seven bedrooms and sits at the base of a ski lodge. Everyone but Eden and Betty Paige will have their own rooms. Each room has a view of either the lodge, the mountain, or the forest. Tons to do there. We can ski during the day, relax, and drink in the hot tub at night. It'll likely snow and will definitely be cold."

Eden is going to throw a fit, but some family time away will be worth it.

"Oh, and the best part—cell service is questionable. Everyone can unplug while we're there."

"I love the sound of this, Josie," Katelyn says. "Count me in. I'll talk to Quinn and see if he and Nola have plans. I don't know if they're heading to her family's plantation or what for the holidays, and I'll call Elle and see if she and Ben want to come."

"And I'll take care of Noah and Peyton. He doesn't have a game, but Peyton might have to work," Josie says.

"Well, the Jameses are in. Eden will have to survive a

real winter instead of begging her dad to take her to Hawaii to surf."

Josie claps her hands together. "You have no idea how happy this makes me. Even if the kids can't come, the six of us . . . well, eight with Eden and Paige...will be together again."

Before we hang up, Josie gives us the dates she's booked the house for, what airports we can fly into, and car rental services. She also tells us she will email all of the info, so we don't have to remember everything or decipher our own chicken scratch handwriting later.

After we hang up, I open the internet on my phone and look up the house. My mouth drops open at the majestic beauty of it all. I can easily see Jimmy and I standing on the deck, sharing a glass of wine, or sitting in the hot tub while snow is falling.

I continue to scroll through the photos, wondering when the last time was that I saw snowfall. Sure, it snowed in Beaumont a couple of times, but mostly flurries. Nothing substantial or anything. We had a blizzard once, but that was so long ago, I think Noah was about nine, which put the twins at four. Since moving to California, we just have hot weather and hotter weather. When it does rain, we rejoice and often stand outside in it, soaking up the drops. I used to do this with Eden when she was little. We'd dance in the backyard and just enjoy the showers. Now she spends so much time in the ocean, when the weather is crappy, she's moody.

The front door slams. I close my app and wait for whoever just arrived home to come into the kitchen, where I spend most of the time unless I'm volunteering or driving Eden to her events. She's old enough to drive and does drive herself to school, but Jimmy and I decided we'd always drive her to her competitions. We still want Eden to know how much we support her.

"Hi, Mum." Eden comes in and kisses me on my cheek.

"How was school?"

Eden goes to the refrigerator and opens it. "Boring, lame. You know, the same."

"Mhmm." I keep my eye on her, watching to see what she'll pull out. Lately, she's been snacking after school and not hungry at dinnertime. For some, this isn't an issue, but Eden would rather be in her room or down at the beach instead of sitting around the dinner table. Neither Jimmy nor I are fans of this kind of behavior.

I smile but duck my head so Eden can't see that I'm pleased with her smoothie choice. She comes over to where I'm sitting, pulls the barstool out, and sits with a heavy sigh.

"What's wrong?" I ask as my hand brushes over her long, chestnut hair.

Eden sighs again dramatically and slouches. I gently push on her back to remind her to sit up straight. For the past couple of years, she's been working with Xander, Harrison's brother-in-law, to build a stronger core. You would think with all the surfing she does, she wouldn't need a trainer, but apparently, to get to the next level, she needs one.

"Stupid girl drama. You know my friend, Zyan?"

Zyan Morgan is Eden's recent crush, and by recent, I mean for the past six to eight months. They met on the circuit when he came here for a couple competitions. He lives in Hawaii with his dad, which is perfect according to Jimmy.

"I remember Zyan," I tell Eden.

"Well, he's moved here."

My insides twist. I can hear Jimmy already, swearing up a storm about that boy coming to the house, especially when we aren't home. "He did?"

Eden nods. "And he didn't even tell me, ya know?"

No, I really don't.

"I'm walking to class and all these girls are giggling by the lockers, so I go see what's so funny. Well it's Zyan and he's just eating up the attention. I call his name and he looks at me like he doesn't remember me and then it hits him and he goes, 'Oh hey, Eden' like we aren't friends and didn't make out all summer long."

"You made out with Zyan all summer long?"

Eden rolls her eyes. "Not the point, Mum."

"Oh," is all I can say.

"Anyway, of course Bentlee and Harmonee were standing there and they knew all about Zyan and me, but today they're all 'So, did you make it up or what?' and they know I didn't, but now they're going around saying Zyan is only an *acquaintance.*"

"I see." I really don't, but for the sake of not going into details with her or asking more about these make out sessions with Zyan, I'm going to just accept I'm out of the loop.

"Yeah, so whatever. And while all this is going on, Rusty asks me out."

I mentally go through the class list from Eden's school, trying to place a young man named Rusty.

"Kira's brother."

"Oh, he's younger, right?"

Eden nods while she takes a drink from her smoothie. "Only by a year, but he's on the varsity baseball team. He plays first base."

"Well, it's nice to be asked out."

She shrugs. "Yeah, I don't know. We'll see."

I wish Katelyn and Josie were here to offer me all the safe advice. Sometimes, I feel like I'm treading water where Eden is concerned or battling Jimmy over what I think she should be allowed to do and not do. I think she should date. She's old enough and definitely mature. She has a good head on her shoulders and is on track to go pro with her surfing. I want her to go to college, and I'm hoping she will, but the circuit can be time consuming and grueling.

"Well, let me know about Rusty, and if you want to talk about Zyan. I've been told I'm a good listener."

"Thanks, Mum. I'm just mad because I thought we had something going on. I guess I was wrong."

Jimmy is going to murder this boy.

"Where's Dad?"

"He's at the tattoo parlor."

"What's he getting this time?"

I laugh because the man is almost out of space. "I don't know, he said it was a surprise."

"Think you can come down to the beach with me for a bit?"

I nod and slide off the barstool. That is another rule we enforce—no surfing by yourself. There have been far too many accidents where someone has gotten hurt and there wasn't anyone around to help them. I don't want Eden in that position—ever.

"I'll go change and meet you downstairs in a few minutes." Again, I brush my hand down the length of her hair. I kiss the side of her head and retreat toward my bedroom. Eden is hot on my heels, only she goes to the right when we get to the top of the stairs and I turn left.

2

JIMMY

Harrison drops me off at the end of my driveway. He doesn't offer to give me a goodbye kiss or tell me he'll call me. To be honest, I'm a little pissed off at how cold and unaffectionate he is. I turn slightly to look at him, and flutter my eyelashes. "When will I see you again?"

He slowly looks my way. I smile and tilt my head to the side. "What the fuck is wrong with you?"

I scoff. "We just had an amazing time, and you're dumping me on the side of the road like yesterday's rubbish."

Harrison chuckles. "I don't know how Jenna puts up with you. Get out of my car before I remove you."

"What an arse," I mutter as I open the door. After I get out, I shut it but keep my hand on the door, bending down a little so I can see him. "Seriously, though, thanks for going with me."

"You said tattoo," Harrison quips. "I'm always up for some ink."

"And yet you didn't get any," I point out.

He shrugs. "But I have an idea for one, so there's that."

I knock my hand on the door and tell him I'll see him later. We're planning to go shopping for the wives and kids later in the week, hoping that we can come up with some inspiration for presents because neither of us have a bloody clue what to get for anyone. It's hard when the people you love have everything they could ever want. I turn towards my home. It's a two-story house with a wooden door and a two-car garage. It's nothing flashy by any means, which was precisely what Jenna wanted. She didn't want a house with a fence or gate where the paparazzi could hang around at all hours of the day or night. She wanted to feel as normal as possible. This house gives my wife what she wants. The best part is the view of the Pacific Ocean at our back door. By all accounts, according to entertainment industry standards, our house would be classed as small, but I don't care. It's perfect for the three of us, and it allows Eden to surf whenever she wants. You'll never see our house in one of those celebrity magazines or on some ridiculous TV show though, and I'm absolutely okay with that. The only thing it does lack is privacy with the neighbors being almost on top of us, but they're cool. Every now and again, Jenna has them over for dinner or cocktail parties where I get to play bartender, which I find amusing. I've even started creating my own drinks, although Jenna doesn't really like them. I should probably take that as a sign that I'm not quite an expert yet.

Inside, the house is quiet, except for the sound of the sea lapping against the shore. Usually there's music playing, the TV is on, or dishes are rattling around, but not today. I walk to the back of the house which is my favourite. There's a wall of bifolding doors which open completely and stay that way most of the year. I do make sure to close them at night or when there's a storm, but it's one of the best parts of our house.

I step out onto the veranda and rest my hands on the railing. Even though it's December, the temperature is higher than normal, but there's a nice breeze, making the day almost perfect. I stand for a minute and watch Eden as she rides a wave back to shore. It's not the best time to surf, but keeping Eden out of the water is not a fight that Jenna nor I are willing to put up with. Eden needs to practice and has the determination to be the best. I can't fault her for trying to achieve her goal.

I'm not sure how long I stand there, but the desire to be with my wife and daughter is far too much to bear. I make my way back through the house and down the steps which lead down to the beach. Luckily, I'm still wearing my combat boots and they easily trudge through the sand.

"Hey, Sweet Lips," I say as I approach Jenna. She turns around and smiles, either because I've used my favourite term of endearment for her, or simply because she's happy to see me. Or maybe it's both, sometimes I can never be too sure. I lean down and place my lips to hers, in need of a kiss.

"What did you get?" she asks when we part. Jenna pats the spot next to her on the blanket, and I happily sit down. I shrug out of my jacket and roll up the cap sleeve of my shirt to show my wife the sugar skull I had inked on my shoulder. It hurt like a bitch, but I'm a man. I can deal with it.

"Wow, white gauze and tape. Very original," Jenna says, laughing.

I roll my eyes and start to peel away the medical tape.

I purposely didn't tell her what I was going to have done because I wanted it to be a surprise. Having said that, I probably should've taken care of this in the house and cleaned my arm ahead of time, so she could see what it was. Too late now. After the gauze is off, I turn ever so slightly so she can see my arm.

Jenna's mouth drops open, and her finger moves towards the freshly-inked spot. "That's my drawing," she says breathlessly. Her eyes meet mine. They're watery, and a single tear spills over her lower lid. "Jimmy."

It's not going to matter what I say in this moment because the likelihood is that whatever I say will not sound as smooth as it does in my head. I'm sarcastic and use humour to deflect from any situation. Instead, I lean forward and press my lips to hers. "I loved it so much," I tell her when we part, "and I always want to remember what it looks like."

"I love it," she says. "And I love you."

We kiss again and continue to do so until a rather aggressive clearing of a throat interrupts us. Without removing my lips from my wife, I side-eye my daughter.

"Seriously, Dad. Ugh." Eden slams her board down into the sand with a huff. "You know, none of my other friends' parents act like this."

"That's because most of them are on their third or fourth spouse."

"Jimmy." Jenna backhands my chest, causing me to flinch, which is her hint that I should tone it down a little.

"I love your mum. You should be happy that we're in love and not fighting."

"I am, just not in public," Eden says. Mind you, we're on a private part of the beach, and there isn't a soul near us.

"Fair enough, Eden," Jenna says. "Are you done? We need to have a family meeting."

Eden's eyes widen dramatically, which makes me think she's done something at school. Dread fills the pit of my stomach. When Eden was little, things were easy. When she started talking, I knew I was in for a roller-coaster ride. She is a walking, talking, Jimmy Junior, which no one should have to experience.

"What happened?" I ask.

Jenna places her hand in mine. I stand and pull her to her feet. "Nothing. We have a proposition to discuss."

I catch Eden's face relax and wonder what was worrying her. It's something I'll have to discuss with Jenna later when we're alone and allowed to make-out without our teenage daughter telling us we're gross. I offer to carry Eden's surfboard, but she declines, which I expect her to do. Long ago, we set the ground rules. Much like my band equipment, I'm responsible for its upkeep and making sure it's always properly stored. I stressed this with Eden and her boards. They're expensive, and she needs to understand the value of them.

Jenna and I hold hands, and Eden walks next to her mum. When we get to our stairs, I stay with Eden while she puts her board away, and Jenna carries on ahead. With Jenna out of earshot, I ask Eden what's going.

"What do you mean?"

"I saw your face back there when Mum said we were having a meeting. Is there something going on that I need to know about?"

Eden shakes her head. "Just girl drama at school is all."

"Okay." I place my hand on her back and walk with her up the stairs. Inside, Jenna has Christmas music playing, and there's a loud racket coming from the kitchen. Eden and I walk in, and I don't know what she thinks when she sees her mum in an apron, but man, my mind goes to places that are definitely rated R.

"I'm making cookies," Jenna says as she takes out the various ingredients from the fridge and cupboards. "Why don't you both sit at the island, and we'll talk while I bake."

"And then we can have a cookie when they're ready?" I ask.

"Duh, Dad. Do you really think Mum would be able to keep us from getting them?"

I eye my daughter suspiciously and finally nod. "You have a point, Little One. Nothing can keep us Davises from freshly baked cookies."

Jenna eyes the both of us while she mixes whatever she's dumped into the bowl with a wooden spoon. Eden grabs a couple of drinks and puts one down in front of the chair I normally sit in. She then goes to the snack cupboard, but Jenna bats her hand away and tells her to sit down.

"Okay, Sweet Lips, what's going on?"

Beside me, Eden mutters, "Gross." I ignore her. It's only recently that she's had a problem with her mother and I showing affection. Jenna says it's a teenager thing.

"Josie, Katelyn, and I had a group call today. Josie has rented a big house in Stowe, Vermont, and has invited us to spend Christmas with them."

"Sounds good to me, when do we leave?" I ask.

"Wait. What?" Eden looks from me to her mum. "We always go to Hawaii for Christmas."

"And this year we're going to Vermont," I tell her.

"That's not fair." She crosses her arms over her chest

and huffs. "Every year we go to Hawaii so I can surf. I look forward to this trip all year long, and now you're going to take it away without even asking if I'm okay with it?"

My jaw clenches, and I see red. The teenage years can't go by fast enough for my liking. I don't remember being this way with my father, but maybe I was.

"Eden," Jenna says calmly. "It's nice to change things up a bit, and we haven't seen Josie and Liam in a while. We miss them. And I suspect you miss Paige. The house is beautiful. Josie is hoping everyone will be there. There's a hot tub on the deck, and you can go skiing."

"What about Quinn? Is he coming?" Eden asks.

Jenna shrugs. "Katelyn was going to talk to him and Nola later today. She isn't sure if they already planned to go to South Carolina for the holidays."

"So, it could just be Paige and me?"

"I mean, it's possible. Josie is hoping Noah and Peyton will be there, at least for a couple of days."

Eden sighs and dramatically drops her head to the counter. My eyes move from my daughter to my wife, and I shrug because I have no idea what to say. I get where Eden is coming from though. For a while now, we've spent the holidays on the beach. I'm not usually one for change either, but I do like the idea of spending time with my friends.

Jenna rubs her hand up and down Eden's arm and tells her everything will work out. Eden clearly doesn't believe her because she melodramatically stands up and tells us she'll be in her room, undoubtedly planning our demise.

"You *do* remember she picks our old folks home, right?"

Jenna goes back to mixing the cookie batter and slaps my hand away when I try to reach for some dough. "She's acting entitled, and I don't like it."

"She's seventeen," I remind her. "And spoiled."

"Well, we knew that was going to happen when she ended up being the only child." Jenna drops her eyes. That was the wrong thing to say. I get up and walk over to her, my arms wrapping around her waist from behind, and pull her to me. "I'm sorry, that was an insensitive thing to say."

"It's fine."

"It's not. We can still try if you want?"

Jenna shakes her head. "Eden is almost an adult. I do not want to start over. I'll just borrow Katelyn and Josie's grandbabies."

I step back and look at my wife. "Wait, is Peyton up the duff?"

Jenna laughs. "Not that I know of, but Katelyn and Josie are eagerly waiting."

"Damn, Liam is going to have a heart attack."

3

JENNA

The one thing I never had when I was growing up was money. My parents worked, and my father often took as many overtime hours as he could or picked up odd jobs on the side to make sure my mom and I had a comfortable life. As a teen, I had a job and learned the value of a dollar. I never whined to my parents that life wasn't fair or stomped my feet when I didn't get my way.

As Jimmy drives toward Santa Monica to the ski shop, I wonder where I went wrong as a parent. Spoiled doesn't begin to describe Eden right now. I know some of it has to do with her environment and the fact that her father is a musician in a successful band, but I can't help but ask myself—where did I go wrong? I suggested to Jimmy and Eden that we rent their ski equipment since this was our first time going. You would think I started the next world war or something with the hand flailing, the dramatics, and the "I have to have the best" comments that followed. Jimmy agreed with her, and I did what I always do, deferred to him. The way I see it, it's his money, and if he wants to spoil her, he can. He's earned it.

Eden is an amazing daughter. She's a straight-A student, focused on a career path, doesn't disrespect Jimmy, and has never done anything for either of us to lose trust in her. So, why am I so upset that she's pitching a fit about going to Vermont for the holidays instead of Hawaii? Deep down, I think it's because it's something I really want to do, and Eden gave me flack about it.

Jimmy pulls into the parking lot, finds a spot farthest away because he doesn't want anyone to ding his Escalade, and shuts off the engine. For a moment, we're silent. Eden's enthralled with whatever song or podcast she's listening to, and my mind is racing. I'm excited to see Katelyn and Josie, to spend hours upon hours with my best friends, but the snow isn't my thing. I hate the cold, especially after living in California for so long. However, I'm willing to brave the frostbite for some fun and relaxation.

The three of us pile out of the car. Eden trails behind Jimmy and me, with her ear pods, plugs, or whatever the heck they're called these days, jammed into her ears. When we get to the double doors, Jimmy stops and turns toward our daughter. He holds his hand out, and she sighs as she drops her phone and ear thingies into his hand.

"Thank you, Little One," he says with a smile. Jimmy has never stopped calling Eden by the nickname he gave her as a baby. To my knowledge, she's never asked him to stop. Even if she did, I don't think he'd listen to her. He likes to use pet names. Mine doesn't bother me in the slightest.

He opens the door for us and ushers us in. I watch as

he and Eden take in the store. I know zilch about skiing or snowboarding and can honestly say I'm not sure I've even been sledding.

"Where do you want to start?" I ask. They're both wide-eyed, and I have a feeling Eden is now a little more receptive to the idea of being on the mountain instead of the beach.

"I want to try snowboarding," Eden tells us. She points to the wall of what looks like mini surfboards but wider than skis.

"That's probably a good idea," Jimmy says. He motions for Eden to go check out the boards, and I follow. I'm here for fashion advice, only. I had planned to stay home and enjoy the quiet, but Eden insisted I come to help her pick out the right outfits.

We're barely at the snowboard section when a young man approaches us. "Dude, no way. My friends are never going to believe this," he says in a surfer dude type accent. I already know what's coming and have long learned to ignore the fangirls and guys who sometimes bombard the guys.

"All right mate?" Jimmy says, shaking his hand and sidestepping that the guy clearly knows who Jimmy is. "We'd like to look at your best snowboards, please."

"Gnarly. Gonna hit Tahoe, Vail? They have the best pow pow."

"Pow pow?" Jimmy questions while I snicker. Jimmy loathes guys like this, who speak in slang. Most of the time, he can't understand the surfers Eden hangs out with and claims it's because he's British, although he's lived in the United States longer than he ever did in England. There have been times when he's straight-up started talking in a cockney accent just to throw Eden's friends off.

"Listen, mate. We're going to Vermont to snowboard. We've never done this shit before, so we need you to hook us up with the best."

"Sick bro. All right, let me show you what we have for you bunnies."

"Make sure they get helmets," I blurt out. Eden's eyes go wide, and I shrug. I tap the top of her head. "Gotta protect the melon."

"Mum!"

Jimmy laughs.

"Brain buckers are a must." The salesman snickers. He starts pointing at boards and saying things that I don't understand. Instead of following them around as they he shows them what they need, I stay near the clothing rack and start looking at snowsuits I think Eden would like. Knowing Jimmy, they'll each get a couple, so they aren't wearing the same one repeatedly. I'm sure the same can be said for the others that will be there.

By the time Jimmy and Eden have been outfitted with boards, boots, and brain buckets—as they're so aptly referred to in the store—they find me deep in the clothing section with a pile of items in my arms.

"You know we're not moving there, right?" my lovely husband points out.

"I know, but I figured you'd want a couple of different outfit options, plus I couldn't pass up these flannel blankets."

"Mum, Vermont is like home to the flannel or something."

"How do you know this?" I ask her.

She looks away sheepishly before making eye contact. "I may have done some online surfing." A small smile creeps across my face, and she puts her hand up. "Stop with the smile. I'm still mad but trying not to be a brat."

I step forward and give her a quick kiss on her forehead. She's not embarrassed by my affection, especially in public, and I'm very thankful for that. "Thank you," I tell her. "Now, let's find you both the right things to wear. I don't want you freezing out there."

"Yeah, because I read it can get to be twenty below zero in Vermont, and people still go outside." Eden shudders. "I don't get it."

"Me neither, but we're going to have a lot of fun," Jimmy says as he takes the pile of clothing I made for him into the dressing room.

ON OUR WAY HOME, we stop at the mall. Always a fun time, said no one ever. When it's Eden and me, it's no big deal. But get Jimmy, the self-professed Twitter God, into a mall with middle-aged women who still scream like banshees when they spot him, and it's a whole other scenario. At the beginning of our marriage, because Jimmy and I skipped the dating part, the fan encounters caused a lot of jealousy issues for me. Mostly because Jimmy was *that* guy—the one who wouldn't think twice about going home with a fan or hooking up with someone he met on Twitter or the mall. Even after our marriage became public knowledge, women still came after him. It still bothers me, but I know Jimmy is faithful. He would never do anything to hurt, dishonor, or put me in a position where I question him.

There's a surf shop in the mall which is our first stop. I find it funny that we even come in here because Eden's sponsors make sure she has the best of everything. Secretly, I think she likes to look to see if there's something she wants but won't outright ask her dad to buy her. Or maybe it's because the guy working is flirting with her.

"What am I witnessing here?" Jimmy asks.

"Nothing," I tell him even though I know he knows what's going on. He's the biggest flirt to walk the streets of Los Angeles. Everyone, it doesn't matter who you are, gets a smile. The truly lucky ones get a picture.

"That bloke is manhandling my daughter."

I glance over to see what he's fussing about. The kid, who is probably a year or two older than Eden is touching her, but he's laughing when he does it, so I'm going to assume either she or he has told a joke.

"They're talking, Jimmy."

"He's trying to talk her out of her bloody wet suit."

I smirk. "Eden's wearing jeans. Probably easier . . ." I don't finish my sentence because I know he'll fly off the handle.

"Not helping, Sweet Lips."

Reaching for Jimmy's hand, I tug him behind me, farther away from Eden. "Give her some privacy."

"She's a child."

"She's almost an adult, Jimmy. You have to let her grow up."

"I tried," he points out. "Don't you remember a few years ago when she wanted to date that bloke from Australia, and he was like eighty?"

"Oh, Jimmy," I say his name with a sigh. My hand cups his cheek, and I smile. "You're going to give yourself a heart attack with all this worry. We have to trust Eden to make good choices. That guy from a couple of years ago was just a first crush, and it went nowhere. He was too old for her, but he wasn't eighty."

"I know guys like him, trust me."

His statement causes me to laugh. "Because you used to be like him, that's why. You probably saw yourself in him, and that's scary for everyone." Jimmy growls and places his hand on hip. He squeezes a bit and then starts to tickle me.

"Stop it," I say through gritted teeth. "We're in public, and our daughter is right there."

Jimmy comes closer and says into my ear, "When we get home—"

"Are you guys ready?" Eden interrupts us, causing Jimmy to pull away. He growls and mutters something unintelligible. I feel bad for him. Sometimes.

"See anything you like?" I ask Eden.

"Nah," she says with a shake of her head. "Most of this stuff I had last year, and it's just now hitting the market. Sort of lame."

Jimmy sets his hand on Eden's shoulder. She allows his hand to stay, which surprises me. Normally, she has a strict no touching policy in public. "Your sponsors take care of you," he tells her. "It's important that you return the favour."

"By winning?" she questions.

He shakes his head. "Winning isn't everything, Little One. It's nice and it's often expected, but your mum and I want you to be the best you can be. The wins will come, just as they have previously."

"I know, Dad. I just want to be number one."

"You'll get there," I say with a wink.

We walk into one of the larger department stores and

head to their winter section, which is scarce. I feel we're going to have to buy a lot of stuff online and end up having to ship it to where we are staying.

The salesclerk comes up to us and asks if we need help. I nod and say, "We're heading to Vermont, and it's cold there."

The clerk laughs. "I used to live there. Cold is an understatement. What are you doing there?"

"We're going to Stowe to snowboard," Eden chimes in.

"You won't find much here to help you, but I can give you a list of places that definitely cater to the weather of New England."

"That would be great," I tell her.

She motions for me to follow her to the register where she starts writing things down on a pad of paper. She rips it off and hands it to me. There are at least ten websites for us to find what we need.

"Thank you."

"Burton is the top choice. Best snowboards and gear, pretty much everything you'll need. North Face too. Even though they're from California, their colder stuff is in the Northeast. L.L. Bean has amazing flannel jeans. I used to live in them."

"You're a lifesaver."

She smiles. "But I would be remiss if I didn't show you what we have here. Let's check out a few of my winter favorites."

The three of us follow the clerk around the store, once again adding items we may or may not need. If we're not careful, we're going to end up taking so much stuff we'll need a caravan to transport everything.

After we check out, Jimmy runs our purchases to the

car and meets us in the food court which isn't my favorite place, but it's convenient, fast, and I'm starving. I just hope that once Jimmy sits down, he'll be able to eat before the fans start clamoring for pictures.

Famous last words.

4

JOSIE

I'm standing outside, admiring my holiday window display, when I hear the sound of a tire rubbing against the curb. It's not the first time I've heard this, and it definitely won't be the last, but it's caught my attention none the less because Liam is giving Betty Paige driving lessons. I think every student driver, at one time or another, has hit the curb outside of my shop. I turn and look into the windshield and laugh at Liam's wide-eyed expression and Paige's scrunched up face.

As soon as Paige turns the ignition off, she and Liam are out of the car and rushing toward me. Both are speaking a mile a minute, and I can only pick up on a few things. I hear words like best day ever, I can't do this, I can't wait to go again, and I need a beer, which definitely came from Liam. I put my hands up; a silent way of asking them to stop.

"Breathe," I tell them. I step forward and kiss Liam. Betty Paige pretends to gag. But she smiles when I pull her into my arms and kiss her on top of her head. I inhale deeply, loving the scent of her shampoo. She's growing up too fast, and I'm desperately trying to hang on to every bit of her that I can.

"Come on into the deli. It's quiet right now. I'll bring us some pie." Liam holds the door for Paige and me. We walk through the flower shop and into the deli, where my assistant manager, Trudy, waves to Liam and Paige. Trudy started working for me after she moved to Beaumont from the big city. She had retired and was bored most days and would often find herself sitting in the deli, reading a book. When I placed the "Now Hiring" sign in the window, she applied and has been a lifesaver ever since. Trudy not only runs the deli but the flower shop as well, giving me more freedom to travel with Liam and be home when Paige needs me. Not that she needs me often. She's a thirty-year-old in a teenager's body. "Needing" Mom or Dad is so uncool right now.

I cut three slices of pie and put each piece on a separate plate—pumpkin for me, apple for Paige, and blueberry for Liam. Paige and Liam get a scoop of ice cream after I heat theirs in the microwave. When I get to their table, they're engrossed an in-depth discussion with fingers moving all over the table. To me, it looks like they've set up an obstacle course with the salt and pepper shakers and the condiment bottles. When I approach, they sit up and each reach for their pie.

"Do you want anything to drink?" I ask before sitting down.

"I'll get whatever you need," Trudy says from behind me. "Sit down, enjoy your pie." I smile and do as she says.

"We're lucky to have her," Liam says before he takes his first bite. "Damn, this is so good." His eyes close as he finishes eating. That's the other thing about Trudy; she can bake circles around me.

"Did you speak to Jenna and Katelyn?" Liam asks.

"I did. Everyone is coming. Just waiting to hear from Noah."

"Can Mack come?" Betty Paige asks. I freeze while Liam chokes.

"Honey, I'm sure Mack wants to spend Christmas with his family."

"And I'm not spending my holidays with Nick," Liam barks out. As if we didn't already know this. I swear, this feud is going to be the death of me. More so, if anything does happen between Mack and Paige, Liam is liable to . . . well, I don't know. There are too many scenarios and possibilities. Liam accepted Nick into Noah's life because he had no choice. I wasn't going to ask my son to forget about the man who helped raise him. Liam gets that. But he's determined to put his foot down where any relationship between Mack and his daughter is concerned.

"Daddy," Paige whines.

"The answer is no, Paige."

"That's so unfair. Noah gets to bring Peyton."

I stifle a laugh at her argument. She uses it anytime Liam tells her no. He sets his fork down and makes a steeple with his fingers. These two butt heads like there's no tomorrow.

"Betty Paige, Peyton is your brother's wife. Of course, he can bring her. Mack, is your friend, who would rather —and I'm just guessing here—spend Christmas with his parents and sister."

She sighs heavily. "Maybe Mack can come after Christmas?"

Liam glances at me, and I shrug. Honestly, we love Mack. He's a great kid and excels at whatever he does. Despite Nick and Liam's issues, there isn't another boy

Liam would rather see his daughter start dating when she's allowed to date—which isn't for another forty years or so.

"If you ask your mother nicely, maybe she'll reach out to Mack's parents and see if we can arrange something."

Paige's eyes go wide, and her mouth drops open. Before she even asks, I set my hand on hers and nod. "I'll ask Nick and Aubrey. If they say yes, you can invite Mack."

"Oh, thank you, thank you, thank you." She bounces up from her seat and tackles me with a hug. She goes over to Liam next and whispers, "Don't worry, Daddy. You're still my number one guy."

When she goes back to her chair, I hand Liam a napkin. "Your eyes are sweating."

He clears his throat and excuses himself. Trudy returns with our drinks. A vanilla milkshake for Paige, a chocolate one for Liam, and coffee for me.

"I made Dad cry," Paige says.

I nod as I take a sip of my coffee. "You gotta give your dad a break sometimes. He doesn't want you to grow up."

"Is it because he missed so much time with Noah?"

Shrugging, I sigh and set my mug down. "One of the reasons, but mostly because you're his baby. Growing up is hard on parents. One day, you're this tiny little thing we carry around, and then you're a walking, talking, sassing teenager. It's like we blink and boom, you're a big kid."

Liam returns, clear-eyed, and with a smile on his face. He sits down, glances at the milkshake Trudy brought him, and starts drinking. Betty Paige and I watch with rapt attention as he sucks on the straw.

"He's going to give himself a brain freeze," she says quietly.

"He deserves it if he's going to drink like that."

Liam gets to the end of the glass and sets it down. He lets out what is undoubtedly a satisfying "ah" and looks at us.

"Feel better?" I ask.

He rubs his stomach and winks. If we were at home, he'd let out a burp, and I'd yell at him for being rude. Thankfully, we're in public, and even though we own the deli, Liam would never do anything to embarrass me.

"Much," he says, going back to his pie. "Okay, let's talk vacation. When are we leaving?"

"Friday morning. Paige is going to miss school. I figured with everyone else coming, we can fly on a commercial airline and let Harrison and Jimmy use the jet."

Liam nods. "I'll touch base with the guys later and check-in. Did you ask my mom?"

"I did, but she's going on a cruise with her friends, and I told her not to worry about us, we'll celebrate when she gets back. She was worried we'd be upset that she made plans."

Liam shakes his head. "Not at all. I'm happy she's found people to socialize with."

The relationship Liam has with his mother, Bianca, is good, but sometimes odd. She's a part of our lives and is very close to Noah and Betty Paige. I talk to her occasionally, but we're not close and never will be. I don't know if I'll ever get over the way she treated Noah and me in those first ten years. Liam knows how I feel and doesn't push me to have some miraculous change of heart. She's good to the kids now, and that's all I can ask for.

"And you said you haven't spoken to Noah yet?"

I shake my head. "I left him a message. I'm hoping he'll call back tonight."

"Does the reservation matter on headcount?"

"No, we have the whole house, and there's enough space for everyone. The house is at the base of the mountain, not far from the lodge, and there's a hot tub on the deck."

"Oh, can I bring my bikini?" Paige blurts out.

"No," Liam says sternly. "Especially if you're inviting Mack."

Paige huffs and then starts to pout. I want to change the subject away from Mack, so I ask, "How was driving?"

Our daughter perks right up. "It was great. Dad let me drive all the way to Allentown and back. I wanted to stop at the museum and see all of his football pictures, but he said no."

"No, huh? It seems like that's your favorite word today." I touch his knee with mine.

"What can I say?" Liam throws his hands up in the air. "No is my favorite word, especially when it comes to you." He reaches across the table and taps his finger against Paige's nose. "Driving went well," Liam adds. "Paige is very aware of her surroundings, and with more practice, she'll pass her test easily."

"Think I can learn how to drive the motorcycle?"

This time it's me who blurts out, "No, absolutely not."

"Why not? Noah learned."

"Not at fifteen he didn't," I counter.

"Well, that's just unfair." Paige crosses her arms over her chest and looks down at the table. After a few minutes, her head rises slowly, and she does everything to hide her smile, but it's no use. "I'm just kidding. I don't ever want to learn."

"Oh, phew," I say. "We'll leave all the motorcycle stuff to your dad and uncles."

"Although, I think Eden knows how to drive her dad's," Paige says.

"JD is reckless," Liam states. "Don't ever do anything he tells you, suggests, or otherwise."

I slap Liam lightly on his arm. "Stop, he's one of your best friends."

Liam winks. "I'm only kidding, except for the part where I say don't do anything he tells you to, especially when we're on vacation. Your Uncle JD has never skied a day in his life. You have more experience than he does."

"Does that mean I can take him on the black diamond slope?"

My eyes widen, and I'm sure Liam's do as well. "Please don't kill your uncle, Paige. Your dad needs him for their next album and tour."

Betty Paige sighs dramatically and holds her hand out over the table. She wiggles her fingers and then eyes her palm. Liam sighs dramatically and then reaches into his pocket. He drops the car keys into our teenaged daughter's hand. "We're going right home," he tells her. Something tells me she has a detour planned, whether he likes it or not.

Liam kisses me, and I tell him I'll see him at home for dinner. Tonight, he's cooking, and it's always a surprise. When he and Paige have left, I clean the table and head toward the back of the deli to wash the dishes. A few minutes later, Trudy comes in.

"You have such a lovely family," she says. She doesn't talk much about hers, even though I've asked plenty of times. She never mentions if she has kids or even grand-children.

"Thanks, Trudy. Are you sure you don't mind working over the holidays?"

"We'll have some of the college kids back. We'll be fine."

I smile softly and thank her. I go back to the flower shop and start picking up the mess I've left from decorating the front windows. I'm putting a box away when I accidentally knock another one over. Papers fall out onto the floor. I squat down and pick up the first one I see, only to fall back onto my rear.

In my hand, I hold the original order Mason placed when he started ordering flowers for Katelyn, in his handwriting. I don't know if the tears come first, the ache in my heart, or the swelling in my throat, but the memory of Mason washes over me. I can't help but think what my life would be like if he hadn't died.

Where would I be?

Who would I be with?

Would Liam have ever come back?

Soon, it'll be twenty years since Mason left us, and yet sometimes it feels like just yesterday.

5

LIAM

The sound of a beer bottle crashing into the bed of my truck doesn't have the same effect as it used to. The shattering of glass from the water tower used to be synonymous with football and friends, with bonfires and girlfriends. Now, I sit up here alone. When Harrison and JD lived in Beaumont, they'd come and hang out with me, crack open a few, and we'd chill. We'd come when I knew teenagers wouldn't be here celebrating on a Friday night after a victory. I know this place holds more in my heart than it does my bandmates, but they were kind enough to indulge in my need to visit it.

The city and I are in a legal battle over this place. About eight months ago, they announced their intent to tear the tower down, clean the field, and construct an office building. I offered to buy it because I know how important this place is to the kids. It's become a rite of passage for the teens of Beaumont. And this place means something to me. It's hard to put a price on nostalgia and memories, but I've definitely tried. The city has rejected each offer, and they have left me no choice but to attempt to have this place considered a landmark. Not far from where I sit, there's a bulldozer, waiting for the green light, and across town, there's a judge who will make his ruling after the first of the year.

Sitting here, on this rickety walkway with my legs hanging off the side, I can't help but think about the last time I sat up here with Mason. It was a couple of nights before I left for college. I was angry with him. I had my choice of colleges, scholarships from every big school out there, but I chose to go where Mason wanted to play. I wasn't done being his quarterback and wanted another four years with him. At the last minute, he decided to go to school with Katelyn and Josie, leaving me high and dry. For the first time in my life, I hated my best friend.

Mason found me here, drinking away my pain and anger, having a self-induced pity party. I told him to fuck off and go to hell. Those were the last words I ever said to my best friend, and they still haunt me every day.

The half-empty beer bottle dangles from my finger-tips from some twenty feet or so in the air. I'm about to let it drop when headlights shine in my direction. My solo act is over. I stand and gather my things when I hear my name. I strain to see who is coming, it's just a shadow, but as he gets closer, I groan loudly, hoping he can hear me.

"What do you want, Ashford?" Josie tells me I need to get over my dislike for Nick. She's right, but it's not some-thing I can stomach. I loathe this man for no other reason than he made a move on Josie in high school and then took my place in Noah's life. Granted, I gave up my right to be in Noah's life when I walked out on Josie, not to mention my former manager Sam had a hand in making sure I'd never know about my son.

Nick doesn't answer but instead climbs the ladder

and sits down. I can be a total dick and leave, or I can think about Noah, and how he'd feel if he found out I left. Noah always wins. I sit back down but make a huge exaggerated show about it. It's childish, but I have yet to grow up when it comes to Nick Ashford.

"To what do I owe the pleasure?"

Instead of answering, he pops the tops on two beers and hands one to me. He takes a long pull from the bottle and then clears his throat. "Josie called. She said Mack is welcome to come to Vermont after Christmas."

"He is," I tell him, even though it's against my better judgment. Again, I have to consider Noah, and Mack and Noah are close.

"That's good. Mack will like that." Nick clears his throat again.

I know I'm going to regret this later, but I ask, "Is everything okay?"

Nick slowly shakes his head. He takes another drink of his beer and then lets the bottle drop to the bed of my truck. "Aubrey is going to South Africa, and she's taking Amelia with her."

"Well, if Mack needs to go with you guys, Noah and Paige will understand."

My sworn enemy turns and looks at me. It may be dark out, but there is no mistaking turmoil on someone's face. "I didn't tell Josie when she called, but uh . . ." He pauses and clears his throat again. "Aubrey is moving."

"Oh."

"I haven't told Noah yet, either. I guess it's odd that I'm telling you of all people, but . . . yeah. My wife wants to move back to Cape Town. I've known this for a while but sort of brushed it under the rug. Mack is excelling in Beaumont and probably has a chance at a scholarship or two. She wants to take it all away, and I can't have that." Nick inhales deeply and then sighs. "I never thought I would be in this position to have to choose my child over my wife, but here I am."

"And Amelia decided to go with Aubrey?"

Nick nods. "A girl needs her mother. Amelia knows she can come back anytime she wants."

"And Mack? How does he feel?"

"He's hurt. Sad. Angry with his mother that she won't reconsider. He doesn't want to leave Beaumont. I think back to when I tried to do this to Noah, right after you came back, and Josie was adamant they stay. She was right. I want to think I'm making the right decision, putting my son's future before my happiness . . . before my *wife's*."

I'm quiet for a minute, thinking of how to say what I'm about to, without sounding like a complete ass. "Do you think it's easier to decide to stay here with Mack because things are over between you and Aubrey?"

"As much as I hate to say it, Liam. I think you're right. Aubrey hasn't been happy for a long time, and I've ignored it. Hell, we don't even sleep in the same room. Most nights, I fall asleep on the couch before going to sleep in the den."

"Is there anything Josie and I can do for you and Mack?" It's another question I regret but ask because of our family ties.

Nick nods. "I feel like I need to go with Aubrey and make sure Amelia is settled. I don't want to wonder if where they're living is safe. Do you think Mack could stay with you while I do this?"

"Yes, of course," I tell him. Some logistics have to be

worked out, like where I'm going to lock Betty Paige away, but that's just semantics. "When will you leave?"

"Aubrey wants to leave when the kids release for winter break. I know you're leaving early. I'll wait until after Christmas."

I shake my head. "Mack can spend Christmas with us. I think Noah would really like that. I know Paige would."

"Are you sure, Liam? I know I have no right asking you to help us."

He has every right. He raised my son for me.

"We're family, Nick. As much as I hate it, my son looks at you as a dad. I'll never ask him to stop." I place my hand on Nick's back. "Are you sure Mack is okay with missing Christmas with you, Aubrey, and Amelia?"

"He already knows his mom and sister are leaving and wouldn't be here. I think spending the vacation with your family will be a good thing for my son."

"Okay, then." I tell him when we plan to leave and that I'll make sure all Mack's arrangements are handled so he doesn't have one more thing to worry about. I also tell Nick to get the address of the place we're staying from Josie so he can send Mack's presents there.

We stay for another hour, not really talking about anything. I stick to my limit of three beers and end up driving Nick home. He could've driven, but the risk isn't worth it. By the time I get home, my wife is curled up on the couch with a blanket over her legs, and our daughter is up in her room, hopefully asleep. However, I'm guessing she's texting with Mack.

Josie smiles when she sees me and sets her book off to the side. I sit down and she puts her legs on my lap, making it easy for me to nestle into her neck. "I love you, JoJo."

"I love you too. Is everything okay?"

I nod against her neck and place a few kisses there. Ever since I met Josie Preston, I have never loved another, and I can't imagine not having her in my life. After a long moment, I finally sit up and look at my wife. She's the most beautiful woman I have ever seen.

"Mack is coming with us."

"Yeah, I know. I talked to Nick earlier."

I shake my head and look deep into her eyes. "He's spending Christmas with us."

"What? Why?"

"Nick found me at the tower. He told me you called. We started talking, and he said that Aubrey is taking Amelia to South Africa. They're moving at the end of the week."

"What?" Josie chokes out.

"Nick said it's been a long time coming. Aubrey wants to go home, but Mack is doing really well at BHS, and he doesn't want to take him away from any opportunities. They're not happy." I pause to kiss Josie. When I pull away, I rub my hand through my hair. "Nick wants to make sure Amelia gets settled. He wants to check out the area Aubrey is moving to and asked if Mack could stay with us."

"And you said yes?"

I nod. "Of course I did. I may not want an Ashford dating my daughter, but I'm man enough to put my issues aside. As much as I hate admitting this, Nick was there for Noah when I wasn't. Nick needs some help, and he came to me which I'm sure it took a lot for him to do. I'm not going to be a jerk about things. Besides, if Noah ends up with us, he'll want Mack there too."

"And Paige will be happy."

I groan and bury my face once again. "I need to lock her up."

Josie pushes on my shoulder and slightly turns so she can look at me. "What if they're soulmates? What if they're just like us?"

"Then, I hope they communicate and don't make the same mistakes I did."

"Liam, we both made mistakes. We were eighteen. I thought I was doing what you wanted."

"Which is exactly what I don't want Paige or even Mack to do. If these two are meant to be together, they need to each follow their own path until they can forge one together. I don't want Paige to give up a future to follow Mack or vice versa. And I definitely don't want her to come home pregnant, without him by her side—still to this day, that haunts me. Learning what you went through because I couldn't communicate my feelings to you—I'll never forgive myself. I don't want that for Paige or Mack. We've been there, JoJo."

She cups my cheek with her hand. "You're a good man, Liam Page. And a damn good father. I'm very proud of you right now."

I smile and tilt my head enough to kiss her palm. "I'm still going to put the fear of God into that young man though, because he and Paige are about the same age when we started having sex. I'll be six feet below the ground before he touches my baby."

Josie laughs. "Ah, there's my husband. I was wondering where he went."

"He took a trip down memory lane, and do you want to know what he found?"

"What?" she asks.

"You." I press my lips to hers and pull the blanket over us. The last thing we need is for the young, impressionable eyes of Betty Paige to see what I'm about to do her mother.

6

JOSIE

From the moment I turned on the lights for Whimsicality, people have come in, buying up all the holiday flowers I have. It seems Liam told "someone" we were heading out of town for the holidays, and that "someone" spread the news. Next thing I know, people are under the impression I'm closing for the rest of the year and are scrambling to get their flowers and centerpieces ordered and picked up before I lock up. I don't know how many times I had to say the shop would still be open before people started believing me. I'm not complaining, but I can't recall a time when I've been slammed from the moment I arrived at work.

I finally get a chance to sit down. Trudy brings me a sandwich and a bottle of water. She sets it on the counter, which causes me to jump up and knock the plate.

"Sorry," she says, unaware she hasn't done anything wrong.

"No, it's fine. There's a piece of paper here I want to save." I hold up the order form and look at Mason's faded penmanship. It's been so long since I've thought about him. There was a time when all I ever did was think about Mason, the impact he had on my life and Noah's, and how Mason's death changed everything. I hate thinking of how Mason isn't with us but can't imagine my life being any different than it is now.

Carefully, I set the piece of paper between two books and leave myself a note to get a frame for it when I return from vacation. I want to save it. I want to remember the young, vivacious man he was when he came in to order Katelyn flowers.

"Something important?" Trudy asks. I forgot she was standing here.

"Sort of, it's more of a memento. Do you remember my daughter-in-law, Peyton?"

"Yes, she's such a lovely young woman."

I nod. "She is. When she was five, her father died in a car accident. I had known him most of my life. He and my husband were best friends, and of course, his wife Katelyn is my best friend," I pause and glance toward the books where I put the paper. "He used to come in and order flowers for Katelyn all the time. They didn't have much money, but he wanted her to have a new bouquet to start her week."

"Memories are a funny thing," Trudy says. "Sometimes, they make us feel warm and gushy, and other times they send us down a path we sometimes don't want to go down."

"And sometimes memory lane isn't the best place to be. Mason's death changed us all."

"How so?"

The story of Liam and I is something I haven't told Trudy. I never saw any reason to. It's been so long and it's not really a big deal anymore that he's back. I sigh and smile. "Liam and I had a rough patch for about ten years. He came home when Mason died, and we found our way back to each other."

Trudy places her hand on my arm and gives me a little squeeze. "Sounds like the perfect love story."

Her statement makes me chuckle. "Oh, it's a love story," I say. "Not sure if it's perfect, but we love each other and have since we were teens."

"I've seen the way Liam looks at you. If that's not love, I don't know what is."

Trudy leaves me to my thoughts, and to be honest, I'm not sure I want to be alone with them. Thankfully, the bell that hangs above the door dings, letting me know someone is here. I take a quick bite of my sandwich and wash it down with some water. Once I'm presentable, I step out from behind the curtains.

"Hi, can I . . . Aubrey, hi." My words stumble. By the look on her face, she knows I'm aware of what's going on with her and Nick. "Hi," I say again.

"I guess you know."

I nod. "Just from what Liam said."

Aubrey scoffs. "I can't believe of all the people he could have told, Nick told Liam."

You're telling me. "Sometimes, people just need someone to talk to."

Aubrey walks around and touches a few of the plants. "You know, I honestly thought he'd run right to you."

"I don't see why he would."

"Because you're the one that got away."

"Aubrey, I'm sure Nick is way past the relationship we had. We're friends and really only because of Noah."

She turns and looks at me. Her eyes are red and bloodshot. It bothers me she thinks I'm anything more to

Nick than a friend. I mean it when I say the only reason we talk is because of Noah. I know Liam would prefer Nick to be a nonexistent factor in our lives. At least, until last night, he felt that way.

"My husband—well soon to be ex—won't leave Beaumont. I hate it here. It's boring and mundane. I want an adventure, freedom."

"Aubrey, you should really discuss all of this with Nick. I'm sure if he knew how you felt—"

"He knows. He won't leave. Won't let Mack leave."

"Mack's in high school. Moving is hard on kids."

"That's what Nick says, but I moved a lot when I was younger. My mother homeschooled me. Taught me what it's like not to have a care in the world. I never had a cell phone or gaming console. I played in the dirt, read books, and helped women tend to their children. I think I turned out pretty well."

Yes, except you're trying to uproot your family because you're bored.

"Nick just wants the best for the kids, Aubrey."

"How do you know? Did he tell you?"

I shake my head and realize I need to keep my mouth shut. I can really only assume according to the time I spent with him and how he was with Noah. According to my son, Nick is a great father to Mack and Amelia, but the only family thing we do is go to Noah's football games. I'm about to excuse myself when I see Nick coming toward the shop. Under any other circumstances, I'd be pleased to see him, but not now. Aubrey sees him and then turns to me.

"Right, just friends." She pushes the door open, and within seconds her finger is in his face. I know I shouldn't watch, but I can't turn away. Nick stands there stoically.

Aubrey's voice rises, and I can almost make out what she's saying. It's now that I busy myself because Nick doesn't need a witness.

When the door opens, I peer around the corner and find Nick standing in my shop. "Hey," I say as I set a bucket of roses down.

"I'm sorry you saw that."

"I'm sorry for what you're going through," I pause and make some random hand motion toward the window, "whatever that is."

Nick sighs. "I told her that Mack is going with you for the holidays, and she instantly accused me of having an affair and said she was going to tell Liam."

"Oh."

"Yeah, no matter what I say. I don't get it. Aubrey's the one who wants to leave, but I'm the bad guy because I won't give up my practice, my coaching job, or yank our son from high school. I'm trying to give him a good, stable life, and she's making me feel like I've done something wrong."

"You haven't, Nick. At least from what Liam said. I just want you to know that Mack is welcome to stay as long as he needs."

Nick nods. "Noah and Peyton offered to take him, but that defeats the purpose, ya know."

"I know. Don't worry; our door is open."

Before Nick leaves, he hands me an envelope. I know it's money, even though we don't need it. I don't try to give it back though, sensing that Nick feels like he needs to do this.

The rest of my day goes surprisingly smoothly. When I pull into the driveway, there's a figure sitting on our front steps.

"Hello, Mrs. Westbury." Mack is coming toward me. He's the spitting image of his dad at this age.

"Hi, Mack. What are you doing outside?"

"Mr. Westbury isn't home, and I didn't want Paige to get into trouble for having me in the house without an adult."

Mack looks like he needs a hug. I'm going to have to find some time later to talk with him. I want him to know he can tell me anything, or at least encourage him to call Noah if he doesn't feel comfortable sharing with me. "That's very respectful of you."

"Can I help you with anything?"

I press the button on my fob, and the trunk opens. "I only have a few bags." Mack takes them both from the trunk and heads toward the house. As I'm about to open the door, Liam's motorcycle rumbles loudly behind us. I smile at Mack and usher him in, and then I meet Liam in the driveway.

He takes off his helmet and kisses me. "Hey, JoJo."

Still, to this day, my knees go weak when he calls me JoJo. "Hey. Mack was on the steps when I got home."

Liam looks toward the house and huffs. "I don't like the idea of them alone together."

"We're leaving in the morning. I can't imagine they'll have any alone time. Did you get a chance to talk to Noah?" I ask.

He nods. "They have a couple of days off. Noah said Peyton already booked a flight for them. Either Harrison or I will pick them up at the airport when they get in. I gave them the address to ship their stuff to."

"Perfect." I lean into him and wrap my arms around his waist. "At least our kids will be there."

Liam kisses me again. "I spoke to JD as well. He's

rather excited to 'piss off in the white shit', I think were his words."

"Oh, boy," I say with a laugh. "I'll have to call Katelyn later and see if she heard from Quinn and Nola."

"What about Elle and Ben?"

"Katelyn was pretty sure they'd be there."

Liam rubs his hands up and down my arms. "Something on your mind?"

I nod. "Last night, as I was cleaning up at work, I found one of the old order forms with Mason's handwriting. It just has me feeling nostalgic. I think I'm going to get a frame for it to at least preserve what's left of it. Maybe give it to the girls."

"I'm sure they'd like that."

Resting my head on his chest, I sigh. I just can't bring myself to say what's on my mind. I hate myself for even wondering where Liam and I would be if Mason hadn't died. "We should get inside."

"Yes, I'm almost afraid to walk in."

"They'll be fine."

Liam and I walk into the house, hand in hand. We find Mack sitting on the stairs, with his stuff in front of him, and Paige nowhere in sight.

"Where's Paige?" I ask Mack. He points to the second floor.

"I think she's upstairs. I put the groceries away and then sat here. I don't want to give you a reason to be angry with me."

My hand squeezes Liam's. That hug I wanted to give Mack earlier is back with a vengeance. I don't want to push him or butt into his life, but the mom in me needs Mack to know he's not alone, especially in the Westbury house. I go over to him and hold my arms out. He falls into them immediately and starts crying.

"It's going to be okay, Mack." I hold him for a few minutes until Liam interrupts us.

"Mack, wanna go out back and throw the ball around?"

Mack's eyes light up. "That would be awesome."

My mouth drops open when I see Liam reach for Mack. He puts his arm around his shoulder and pulls him close. I follow a few steps behind them and hear Liam say, "I'm happy you're here, but please don't disrespect my rules."

"Yes, sir. I promise."

7

HARRISON

I'm almost to the house when Katelyn's name displays on the screen. I tap the notification and listen to the artificial intelligence read Katelyn's message aloud. She wants me to meet her at one of our favorite restaurants. A little hole in the wall Mexican place, as it's often described, with the best brisket flautas I have ever tasted. The best part, the paparazzi never seems to come in, which means Katelyn and me, and sometimes JD and Jenna can enjoy a nice quiet meal without someone bothering us for a picture. Autographs are rarely asked for these days because it's all about the 'gram and how many likes you're going to get.

After turning the SUV around, it takes very little time to arrive at the restaurant. As soon as I open the door and step in, Katelyn is there. I smile at the love of my life and make my way toward her. Rosa, the third-generation owner, hollers out, "Hola, Mr. Harrison."

"Good evening, Rosa."

"I'll be over in a minute for yours and Ms. Katelyn's order."

When I reach Katelyn, she tilts her head up, waiting for a kiss, and I happily oblige her. "This is a delightful surprise," I say as I sit down across from her. I don't bother with the menu because I order the same thing every time I'm here.

"I was at the hospital and left late. Figured we'd stop here for dinner."

"Well, you know I'm always up for Rosa's cooking," I say this as she approaches our table. She blushes and sets our drinks down in front of us.

"Mr. Harrison, you sure know how to make a woman feel good about herself."

"He does have that charm," Katelyn says with a sigh and smile.

Katelyn and I place our orders, and I reach for her hand. My thumb plays with the diamond on her ring finger, moving it back and forth. People, mostly the media, often ask why we've never married. I suppose for some people it's odd. We adopted each other's children, took each other's names, and have always acted like we're married. There have been many times when I've referred to her as my wife, and she has called me her husband. So, why not make it official? People want to know, and the answer is a piece of paper does not define our love for each other or the life we're living, or the lives of our kids. The bottom line, this works for us, and that's all that should matter. If something happened to me, Katelyn's taken care of, as are the kids and any future grandchildren.

"You look troubled."

Katelyn smiles softly and leans forward to rest the elbow of her other arm on the table. "There are a few things I'd like to discuss."

"I'm all ears."

"Josie, Jenna, and I had a video chat today," she pauses, which I take as an opening to say something sarcastic.

My mouth drops open. "What did Liam do now?" The likelihood that he did anything wrong is so far-fetched, it's laughable. For the past, however many years, that boy has been on the straight and narrow, and he took JD and me right along with him.

Katelyn rolls her eyes and lets out a small giggle. "Josie has invited us all, kids included, to go away for the holidays. She rented this massive lodge that will fit us all comfortably. According to her, the house sits at the base of the mountain, right by the ski lodge. The Davises are going, and I told Josie we'd go as well."

"I'm game. When do we leave?"

"End of the week. We'll fly to Vermont."

"The land of Ben & Jerry's, maple syrup, and cider donuts. I'll be one happy man." I lean back and pat my stomach.

"You'll be fat if you eat like that."

"And you'll still love me," I point out. Katelyn gives me a side-eye glance but doesn't confirm she will. Her avoidance of my statement hurts a little bit. "What about the kids?"

"Josie is going to call Noah and Peyton. I'll take care of Quinn and Elle. I'm not sure if Quinn and Nola are going to her parents' or not. We really hadn't talked about the holidays."

"That's a bit odd for you. Normally, you know everyone's plans before Thanksgiving. What's going on?" Over the past few weeks, I've noticed something has been on Katelyn's mind, but each time I've asked, she's brushed me off, saying it's nothing. The thing is, I can't fix the issue if it's nothing, and the last thing I want is for Katelyn ever to have to worry about anything. I tug slightly on her hand to get her attention. "Talk to me."

Katelyn inhales deeply. "I'm fine, I promise. The kids are as well. But there is something I want to show you after we eat."

"Okay," I say without hesitation.

As if on cue, Rosa is back with our food and a loud growl bellows from my stomach. I don't bother trying to cover it up with my hand or even apologizing. It knows what I'm about to feed it.

"Plates are hot," Rosa says as she sets them down. "I'll get you some more drinks." I rub my hands together and pick my fork up.

"You act like you haven't eaten all day," Katelyn says.

"I've been with JD, which means we ate at In-N-Out Burger. He's like a kid with a sugar high when it comes to that place."

"Which I don't get. It's not like Jenna tells him he can't go."

I shrug. "It's JD. Who knows with him?"

"What did he get for a tattoo?" Katelyn asks.

"One of Jenna's drawings of a sugar skull. He did it as a surprise."

"That's very sweet of him."

I stifle a laugh because sweet and JD do not go together in a sentence. Although, when it comes to Jenna and Eden, he's an entirely different person.

When Rosa arrives at the table with our bill, I have my credit card out and ready for her. She takes it and tells us she'll be right back.

"Make sure you leave her a good tip since we won't be back until next year."

"Of course," I reply. "As if I'd do anything different when it comes to Rosa."

When she returns, Rosa sets the slip down with a pen and walks away. "How much are you leaving her?" Katelyn asks.

I don't bother to answer her and write the total, plus tip onto the piece of paper and scribble my name. Katelyn takes it from me, writes on it, and hands it back. I say nothing, as I get up and reach for her hand to help her out of the booth.

"Merry Christmas, Rosa," Katelyn says as we begin to leave. "We'll see you next year."

"Next year? What?" Rosa yells out, but we're already at the door. With Katelyn's hand in mine, I look down at her and smile.

"She'll be happy."

"Rosa's good to us." And we're good to her. We always make sure to tip above the normal and more so during the holidays. "A two-thousand-dollar tip will help her tremendously."

"You're a good woman, Katelyn."

She stops and pulls me to her. I don't hesitate to kiss her, not caring if someone has their camera out. Please blast this all-over social media with the caption, "Harrison James kisses his wife on the street corner." So scandalous.

I open the car door for Katelyn and make sure she's situated before closing it. The plan is to leave her car and come back and get it after she takes me to this super secretive place. Once I'm in the flow of traffic, Katelyn is giving me directions. She points to the right or left, but the best is when she says, turn here, and I'm stuck in the middle lane.

"Advance warning, babe."

"I know, I'm sorry."

Clearly, wherever we're going and whatever is on her mind is weighing heavily on her. I hate that for her and want to relieve her of what she's feeling. When she tells me to turn into the hospital entrance, I figure it's to turn around, but she directs into the first open spot she sees.

"Follow me," Katelyn says as she gets out of the SUV. I do as she requests and fall in step behind her. The hospital is busy, with an influx of people milling around. Honestly, it's my least favorite place to be, and I start to wonder if Katelyn has befriended a fan of 4225 West and their dying wish is to meet me. I find this odd because Katelyn would've said something, and I definitely would've made sure the fan received the full treatment.

We step into the elevator with a few other people, and Katelyn presses the sixth-floor button. We ride in silence until the doors open for us and step out. At the nurse's station, Katelyn checks us in. I'm given a sticker that says visitor with my picture on it.

"What are we doing here?" I ask.

"You'll see." Katelyn motions for me to follow, and I do. We walk through a set of double doors that Katelyn opened with her badge and around the corner. She stops at the large window and sighs.

Babies.

"Did someone have a baby that we know?"

Katelyn shakes her head and again motions for me to follow her. We go into the nursery, and she greets one of the nurses, who introduces herself as Mary.

"Are you here to see Baby John?"

Katelyn nods and takes my hand. Being in a place like this, full of babies, is something new for me. I wasn't there when Quinn was born and obviously the twins. Katelyn and I never considered expanding our family either and are both anxious for grandchildren.

"Sit here," Katelyn says as she points to a rocking chair. I do and keep my eyes on my wife. She goes to one of the cradles and scoops up a baby wrapped in a hospital-issued blanket with a blue hat on. Katelyn sits next to me and, for a moment, is entirely focused on the baby she's holding.

"I don't know how long I've volunteered here. It's probably going on two years now. I love coming in and holding the babies and helping the new moms. This job or whatever you'd call it has been rewarding. When I leave, I know the babies are loved, and the parents are walking out with their bundles prepared for sleepless nights. When I go home at night, I'm content and ready to bug Peyton and Noah for a grandchild."

Katelyn gently places the baby she's holding into my arms. I'm nervous but not afraid because I know my wife is by my side. I look down at the little guy and take in his features. He's tiny with blue eyes and the smallest nose. He wiggles and squirms, almost as if he's trying to break out of his swaddle.

"What's his name?"

"He doesn't have one."

"Why not?" I ask, without taking my eyes from him.

"His mother abandoned him at the fire station a week ago. He's been here because the state is having trouble finding him a home so close to Christmas. They call him Baby John because they don't know who he is."

Instantly, my eyes go to Katelyn. She tries to smile,

but there are tears in her eyes. "Why are we here, Katelyn?"

"Because I want us to foster him and eventually adopt him."

"Katelyn," I say her name as a warning.

She sets one hand on me and the other on the baby. "I get it, our kids are grown and hopefully starting families of their own soon, but this guy, he doesn't have a chance. He'll live in a foster home until he's adopted—if he gets adopted. He's small for his age. A full-term baby should weigh at least six pounds, he's barely tipping the scale at five. He may or may not have health issues the older he gets and right now he needs oxygen to breathe at night before he forgets to do it himself. We can take care of him and give him a good life. Give him a chance. We can make sure he has the best medical care."

I glance back at the baby and swear he smiles at me. I haven't thought about more kids since the twins were probably eight. It just didn't make sense. Not with the band touring all the time, and the kids pulling Katelyn in every direction possible. She's right though. We have something to offer a baby.

"We leave on Friday," I point out.

Katelyn nods. "Which means we need an emergency hearing giving us temporary custody of him and listing us as his foster parents until we can proceed with the adoption. I've already spent time with his caseworker. Ramona thinks we have an amazing chance of becoming his foster parents. If we can't take him out of the state, I'll stay home. All we can do is ask."

"And what if his mother comes back?" I ask her. "We've been down this road with Alicia. It's not pretty."

"No, it's not, but if she does, we'll help her, because I

can't imagine Elle or Peyton being so scared that they'd leave their baby at the fire station. I hate that his mom went through this alone. If she comes back, we'll be there for her."

I study my wife for a long time, looking for any signs of apprehension. I finally lean over and kiss her. "After I'm done holding him, I'll make the call to our lawyer."

"Are you sure?" she asks hesitantly.

"I am." Katelyn's eyes go wide and brim with unshed tears. Her hand covers her mouth as I nod, sending the message home. I'll do whatever I must to make her happy, and if that means bringing this little boy home, who desperately needs a family, then so be it. Starting over as parents isn't ideal, but I feel as if this is the right thing to do in my heart.

"I love you, Harrison. So much." She leans down and kisses me. Her long hair tickles against the bundle in my arms. He fusses, which sends a welcoming jab to my heart. We were meant to be in each other's lives.

"I love you more. We should probably think of a name for this guy. I'm not a fan of John."

"Oh, don't worry, I have a list," she says as she places her arm around my shoulder and leans in. I watch her for a moment, wondering if this was how she was with the twins, and can't believe it's taken us this long to expand our family.

8

KATELYN

Harrison and I stayed at the hospital until we had to leave due to visiting hours being over. He wanted to change the bassinet's placard to read "Baby boy James," but the nurse wouldn't let him. That didn't stop Harrison from telling the baby that he would be back, and then he'd have a real name. The entire way home, I cried. Not because I was sad, but at the prospect of helping Baby John have a decent life, and also at the thought of two, three, and four in the morning feedings. I know I'm out of practice but eager to wake up and hold that baby boy and rock him back to sleep.

"Are you nervous?" Harrison asks. We are in the Child's Protective Services office, waiting to speak with Ramona. Before she's even willing to push our request through, she has to meet Harrison.

"I am." I know getting the baby is a long shot, but it's my hope since other foster placements have declined, that we're seen as the only viable option for Baby John.

"We're good people, Katelyn. We have a lot to offer a baby."

"I know," I say quietly. I glance quickly at the man sitting next to me. He's dressed in a suit, with a blue button-down shirt. On the outside, he looks nothing like the man I'm madly in love with. Hidden are his tattoos, the real Harrison James. He rarely dresses like this, but I appreciate every aspect of the incredibly sexy man he is when he does. He catches me staring and winks.

When the door to the offices opens, I look over and smile when Ramona appears in the doorway. She waves us to her. "How are you?" she asks.

"Nervous," I tell her. "Ramona, this is my husband, Harrison."

"It's nice to meet you," he says, shaking her hand.

"You too." She flips through a file as we follow her down an aisle way. On each side of us, gray cubicles make up tiny offices. Most of them have boxes stacked on top of each other, and piles of folders take up desk space. I have a feeling each one of those manila files is a child needing a home.

Ramona takes us to a conference room. It, too, is crowded with boxes and filing cabinets. She tells us to sit. "I've been looking over your application," she starts, and my heart drops. "You're not legally married, correct?"

"No, ma'am," Harrison says.

"We've been together for over twenty years, and you can see by the paperwork I gave you, we adopted each other's children many years ago, without any issues." I know I'm rambling. I can't help it. I feel like she's caught us in a lie. If California would acknowledge common law, we'd be all set. Harrison gives my hand a reassuring squeeze. If never getting married comes back to bite us in the ass, I'm dragging him to the nearest chapel and marrying him.

Ramona looks up. Her face shows little to no expression. I'm sure she's mastered this look over the years. I'd give anything to see what she looks like when she's delivering good news. My palms start to sweat, and my heart races faster than I knew possible.

"You amended your application to include out of state travel?"

Harrison clears this throat. "Yes, we are flying to Vermont on Friday and wish to take the baby with us. If possible," he adds.

Ramona nods.

I want to know what the nod means. Is Ramona agreeing? Is she acknowledging Harrison? Or is she nodding because that's what she's used to doing? Right now, I feel like this isn't the same person I met at the hospital, the one who was eager to get our paperwork started and felt like we had a good chance at becoming foster parents.

Ramona closes the folder and sets her clasped hands on top of it. "Katelyn, I'm going to repeat what I've already told you for Harrison, so he has a clear understanding of how we proceed."

"Okay."

"Approximately, seven days ago, the child known as Baby John Doe 1096 was abandoned. Hospital staff determined he had been born no longer than eight hours prior. Under state law, the birth mother or father had the legal right to leave the said child at a safe haven location without being questioned. They filled out a simple sheet of medical information." Ramona pulls a sheet of paper from the folder and slides it over to us. "More often than not, places are left blank, which leaves us in the dark."

Harrison picks up the paper, and I lean in to read

what's on it. The only ink stain on the sheet is a check-mark next to boy.

"The hospital ran a series of tests, and we can confirm Baby John is not addicted to anything, just underdeveloped and likely premature. An ambulance transported him to the hospital from the fire station, where he has remained under the staff's care. Now," Ramona sighs. "It is my understanding that you wish to foster this child?" She opens her folder and starts writing on a legal pad.

"Yes," Harrison states.

"And you're able to provide a stable home for him?"

"Without a doubt," he replies.

"Tell me about this vacation you're taking? Will Baby John be cared for?"

"As Harrison said earlier, we're going to Vermont. We're staying in a lodge in the town of Stowe and meeting up with our life-long friends, who would play an important part in Baby John's life if we were to adopt him. Our grown children will be there as well. We'll celebrate the holidays as a family."

"And Baby John would be incorporated in all of this?" she asks.

Harrison chuckles. "We'll have six women to fawn over him. I can tell you he won't lack attention."

Ramona actually chuckles at this. "You mention adoption. Is this your intent?"

Harrison and I nod. "It is," I say. "We already know what it's like when a birth parent comes back. We had to experience it with our son, Quinn. We are prepared for Baby John's mother or father or both to return. It's something we're willing to accept."

Her hand moves quickly across the sheet of paper, writing in flowy cursive from what I can tell. I only wish I could lean forward and see what she's putting down. Ramona closes the folder and, once again, clasps her hands together and sets them down. "Normally, I would need a home visit and some time to check your references. Under the circumstances, with time being limited and the holidays approaching, I will put that off until after the first of the year. Mr. James, you are a very public figure, and I can't imagine you're going to fly out of the country with the baby. Therefore, I'm going to sign-off on this foster arrangement temporarily. After I print the necessary paperwork, you'll be able to pick Baby John up from the hospital."

Ramona stands and exits the room, leaving Harrison and me there, stunned. He bumps my arm with his elbow and waits for me to look at him. "I'm thinking you better get on the phone and start reserving a car seat because we're going to need one."

My eyes go wide. "Oh, my God."

"I know." He smiles. "We'll go pick him up, and then we'll go to the store to get everything else. He's tiny, so he'll sleep in our room. You should make a list of everything we'll need."

It's as if I'm on autopilot when I pick my phone up and open my notes app. I start typing everything I can think of from bottles to blankets. It's been so long since I've had a baby, it's hard to remember what they need to survive.

After what seems like an hour, Ramona is back with a mountain of paperwork. At first, Harrison is hesitant to sign anything without his lawyer reading it, but after they talked last night, he said the documents wouldn't contain anything out of the ordinary. Harrison scribbles his name on each line, and I follow. When we're done, Ramona hands us a copy, along with her card.

"Call me if there are any issues."

"There won't be," I tell her.

She shows us which documents we should keep handy and cautions us on getting attached. "The parents have seven days left to in which they could change their mind. If that happens, you'll hear from me."

"But we'll be out of town," I tell her.

Harrison grips my hand with his. "We can fly back. It'll be okay."

I don't know how he does it, but his words calm me. "We'll be okay," I repeat, changing his words slightly.

I'm in tears by the time we reach our car. Harrison holds me in a tight hug while my tears soak his dress shirt. "I hope these are happy tears," he whispers into my ear. I nod against his chest but am unable to look at him. "That's good because, by tomorrow night, they might be tears of frustration if the baby won't sleep."

I lean back enough to look at Harrison. "I'll never get frustrated with him."

Harrison kisses me on the tip of my nose, then my forehead, and finally, the top of my head. "Come on, let's get to the store and pick up a few things for this bundle of joy and think about a name because once we tell JD that the baby's name is John Doe, he'll start calling him JD Jr., and I can't have that."

I snort and cover my nose. "You're right. He needs a name, even if it's just something we call him."

Every thirty seconds of our drive to the store, we're blurting out names. Not a single of one stands out. "I think we need to stop name associating. Saying we know someone or went to high school with someone with that name isn't going to help us," I say as Harrison pulls into the parking lot.

"You're right. Maybe we should call him something that is a mix of Quinn, Elle, and Peyton."

I slowly unbuckle and stare at Harrison. He shrugs. "It's a good thing Quinn is a respectable name."

Harrison laughs and gets out of the car. We meet around the front, and he reaches for my hand. "It's not like I would name my children rocket ship or drumstick."

"You might if given a chance."

As soon as we walk into the store, Harrison is recognized instantly. He doesn't stop and greet the whispers as we're on a mission. When we come to the baby section, I'm overwhelmed.

"Holy crap, how do we pick?" I ask as Harrison pulls his phone out of his pocket and starts typing. "What are you doing? Don't tell anyone yet about the baby. I want to surprise them."

"I'm looking up the best car seat on the market."

"Oh." I start to browse and find a soft blanket, a couple of outfits, and a diaper bag I like. Harrison wanders off, and when he returns, he's pushing a box with his foot.

"Found one."

"Perfect." I show him what I have in my arms. "Can you think of anything else?"

"Nope. We can come back after we pick him up. There's a stroller we're going to grab on our way out. It's a bassinet type. It's cute. I like it."

"And impractical," I tell him. "We need one that fits the car seat."

Harrison shrugs. "Eh, I like this one. He can have two. Also, I found a crib. It's black and awesome."

"Harrison," I groan, but he smiles. He kisses me quickly and says, "Black is manly, and our little guy needs all the confidence-boosting he can get. You can decorate his room in whatever as long as he has a music corner and a black crib. Deal?"

I roll my eyes, knowing I can't win all the battles. "Deal. But I get the final say on his name. I don't want to call this baby Elquinton or something like that."

"Wow, babe, did you think of that name right now?"

"Let's go, Harrison. I want to get him home and snuggle."

"Me too," he says. "Me too."

9

HARRISON

I remember the day Quinn arrived on my doorstep, all I had was a motorcycle. A cheap one at that. I had to use my mom's car, which wasn't anything fancy or safe by today's standards, and my sister, Yvie, often had it. The band had just started getting a sizable following and our records sold, but management pocketed most of the money back then, so I bought a run-down four-door that barely fit Quinn's car seat. This car lasted a month or two before I invested in an SUV, something big enough to protect my son.

Today, I don't have that issue.

When Katelyn and I arrived at the hospital, it was business as usual. I followed her to the nursery, where we found Ramona meeting with the nurse I had met the day before. Both women smiled softly, and the nurse told us to go on in and get the boy. Right then, I hated the way she said "the boy" because I already started considering him my son, which according to the rules of fostering, thanks to the internet, you shouldn't get attached. I'm supposed to disassociate and remember he belongs to someone else, but I can't. From the moment Katelyn told me she wanted to bring him home, to make him a part of our family, giving him the title of "son" is all I've thought about.

I let Katelyn lead and stand by in case she needs a hand. She's a natural at getting our baby dressed. She talks to him in a low voice, coos at him, and gently rubs her fingers over his soft skin. He reacts to her, lifting his small cheek in an attempt to smile. Still, I can't get over how small he is, and I don't remember Quinn looking so fragile, so delicate. Katelyn dresses him in one of the outfits she picked out at the store and asks Ramona to take our picture.

"Yes, but you can't post it on social media," she reminds us.

"I know," Katelyn says.

We pose and smile for a few photos, and then Ramona hands Katelyn her phone back. "It's your first official family photo," she says. I don't miss the words she's used. She, too, must feel like we have a green light to adoption. Those words give me hope.

"No, that'll come tomorrow when he meets his brother and sisters, aunts and uncles, and cousins," Katelyn says as she looks at the baby. "Yes, that's right, my little man. You have a big family waiting to meet you."

"We should go," I say as I put my hand on Katelyn's lower back. "We need to get back to the store and call the kids." Katelyn nods and continues to look at the bundle in her arms. I can't blame her. I'm mesmerized by him as well. She sets him down in his car seat, which seems far too big for him, even with the support piece I installed out in the parking lot. The nurse comes over after Katelyn has buckled him, checks the restraints, and gives us the instructions for his oxygen tank. Honestly, this part is makes me nervous. What if I give him too much or not enough? And what if the oxygen isn't enough for him at night and he needs medical attention? Is he going to be strong enough to cry and let us know?

"I'm going to miss you," she says to him. "You're all set. Does this mean you won't volunteer anymore?"

Katelyn shakes her head. "No, I'll still come a couple of days a week, once we get settled and in a routine."

The nurse smiles. "I look forward to updates."

When given the all-clear, I grab the handle and remember how cumbersome and awkward car seats are. "You'd think someone would come up with a better system," I mumble as we walk out of the nursery. We come around the corner, toward the nurse's station, and everyone has gathered there. They're clapping, not for us, but for Baby John Doe because he's going home. Katelyn hugs a few of the women and promises to bring him back after we've returned from vacation.

"I'm going to sit in the back with him," Katelyn says when we reach the car. "Just in case." I don't need to ask what the just in case is for. I've been there. Quinn hated his car seat. Each time I'd buckle him in, he'd scream, and I would think I had pinched his leg, or the straps were too tight and hurting him. Trial and error. It's how new parents learn, and I quickly figured out it wasn't the car seat making him cry. It was because he liked to be held. Between my mom, sister, and me, we held Quinn every chance we could.

After I snap the car seat into the holder—which is the best invention ever—I stand there for a moment and remember how cramped Quinn was in our first car and how this little guy takes up hardly any space. Katelyn situates herself next to him and starts talking to him right off.

"He needs a name," I remind her. We've narrowed the list down to two names, and I like both of them.

"I want the kids to meet him first," she tells me. A family affair, I get it. When I first saw Quinn, who didn't have a name when his mother left him with me, his name came right to me. This little man in my backseat, I can see him with both of the names we've picked. Sadly, until he's ours, he'll be Baby John Doe and whatever number the state issued him.

After a long and exhaustive trip to the mall, the car is fully loaded with every baby item Katelyn and I could find. We decided while shopping, if the birth mother is to come back, we'll give her everything to help her get started. I asked Katelyn if she were sure about that, and she said yes.

While Katelyn and the little man continue to bond, I put together the cradle we bought and set it up in our room. When we get back from vacation, we'll have one of the spare rooms turned into his nursery, with a fresh coat of paint and all the wall decals we can find. By the time I've finished, my stomach is growling.

"Hey, babe," I say as I come into the living room. She holds her finger up over her lips, telling me to be quiet. Having a newborn in the house is going to be an adjustment for sure. Katelyn sets the new man in her life down into the portable crib and meets me in the kitchen.

"Are you hungry?" she asks.

I nod and lean down for a kiss. "Let's order take-out. We still have to pack, and I want to call the kids."

"I don't want to tell them just yet. Elle will rush over

here, and then Peyton will be upset that she's not here to help."

"I was thinking more like having them meet us someplace tomorrow so we can arrive at the lodge as a family."

Katelyn smiles. "I like that idea. You go call, and I'll order dinner."

We kiss again, but this time it's longer. I had big plans for us tonight, but it looks like those moments with my wife might have a schedule. It won't be the first time we had to get creative.

I head outside, the winter air is crisp and chilly, and close the sliding glass door behind me. I don't want the baby to cry and alert the kids. After pulling up our group chat, I press the video button and hold the phone up, slightly away from my face. While I wait for them to pick up, I make funny faces to entertain myself.

"Will you stop?" I can hear Quinn before I can see his face. The twins appear next, both with odd looks on their faces.

"I get bored waiting for the three of you to answer."

"Dad, it's literally seconds from when you hit the button. You can't be that bored," Elle adds.

"Hi, Dad," Peyton says. Noah is waving in the background but disappears from the frame.

"Peyton, you are officially my favorite," I tell the group. Quinn and Elle roll their eyes. "Okay, your mom says you're all flying to Vermont tomorrow, right?"

The collective sound of three yesses is music to my ears.

"Perfect. Here is what I want to do. I'd like for Peyton and Noah to fly down here tonight and rent a room at the Hilton by the airport. I'll organize the jet if need be. The rest of you, I want you to meet your mom and me at the hotel in the morning. We'll fly as a family to Vermont."

"It'll just be me," Elle says. "Ben is going to his mom's for Christmas."

"Bummer," Quinn says. "Nola isn't thrilled with the idea of snow and has vowed to stay in the lodge drinking wine."

I laugh because I'm sure she's not the only one. "Your mom will happily sit with her by the fire. Did you look at the pictures of the house we're staying in?"

"Noah isn't skiing either," Peyton adds.

"Is that your rule or a team rule?" Quinn asks.

"Team rule," Peyton says, laughing. "If he breaks his leg or arm, he's screwed, and his contract is coming up for renewal."

Elle chimes in with, "Maybe you guys can finally move to California for good."

"His contract is up, not mine," Peyton laughs and reminds her sister.

"Ugh," Elle groans and rolls her eyes.

"Anyway," I interrupt the kids. "Back to the plan. Are we good with it?"

"Yes, but Noah can't leave tomorrow because they have to practice all week, which is stupid but needed. But I'll be there in the morning."

"Not that I'm complaining, but why are we all traveling together now?" Quinn asks.

I sigh and form what I want to say in my head. "Your mom and I have a surprise for you, and we want to give it to you all at the same time."

"Well, I'll be there," Elle says. "Maybe I'll just drive to the house tonight."

"No!" I blanch, much to Elle's surprise. "It's just, you

know . . ." I let my sentence trail off and watch the faces of my children morph into disgust. I can't help but laugh.

"Dad, that is so gross. I don't want to hear about you and Mom." Quinn shudders.

"Yeah, yeah. You're all adults. Get over it." We finalize the details for the morning and hang up. My next call is to Liam, who graciously picks up on the second ring.

"What's up?" he says.

"I thought I'd check and see what time you have the plane booked for?"

"We're not using it. Figured we'd leave it to for you and JD."

"Awesome, perfect. Katelyn and I have a surprise for you guys tomorrow."

Liam laughs. "Oh man, I don't even want to guess. Do you need me to pick you up at the airport?"

"Nah, I'll rent something when I hang up with you."

"Sounds good. I'm bringing my guitar. We can jam. There's a bunch of pubs in the area. I figure we can do a gig or two."

"I'm game. Okay, I gotta call JD and see what his plan is."

"Don't worry about it," Liam says. "JD and Jenna are already there. They went a day early because he went overboard on snow gear and couldn't wait to test it out."

"Typical."

"Pretty much."

Liam and I hang up, and my next call is to the hangar to get everything set up for tomorrow. After this, I call the hotel and book the necessary rooms for the kids. The last thing I want is for them to have to pay for their rooms since they're accommodating their mother and me in our little request.

By the time I have everything set, take-out dinner is sitting on the table, and Katelyn is holding the little guy in one arm and eating with her free hand. I go to her, kiss her forehead, and then lean down and press my lips to the baby. I inhale deeply and take in his baby scent.

"Are we all set for tomorrow?"

"We are. Nola is the only extra flying with us. Noah has practice, and Ben is going to his mom's."

Katelyn looks at me, and her mouth drops open slightly. "Ben is going to his mom's?"

I shrug. I find it odd as well, but it's not my place to say anything. "I guess."

"He didn't come here for Thanksgiving, either."

"He doesn't have to spend every holiday with us," I point out.

"Since when?" Katelyn counters. "When we lived in Beaumont, he was at our house for everything. I just find it odd that he's suddenly going to his mom's."

"Well, I'm sure he has a good reason." I set my hand on top of hers and squeeze it. "Let's eat, and not worry about why Ben has decided to spend Christmas with his mother and get packed. With this little guy, we have a lot of extras to take with us, and I don't want to be in a strange town, not knowing where things are if he needs something."

"You're right." Katelyn smiles and goes back to eating. I make sure her drink is full and find myself begging to hold the baby while I can because once his sisters, aunts, and cousins get a hold of him, I likely won't get to hold him again until the new year.

10

KATELYN

I rest my head on the doorjamb and close my eyes. I underestimated what a two a.m. feeding meant, and the three in the morning diaper change, and the four-thirty wails because the baby was uncomfortable in his new surroundings. Each time I got up with him, even though Harrison woke as well. I know he would've gotten up if I asked, but I felt like it needed to be me. I think because I feel like I've interrupted a routine this little boy had already started to establish at night. And I'm the one who took him away from his night nursing staff.

Harrison rests his hand firmly on my leg, and my hand moves to his in an instant, clutching it tightly. I love this man more than words, and if it wasn't for him, I'm not sure where I'd be in life. I look over at him. He's focused on the road, keeping a steady pace with the traffic. We're on our way to the hangar, where our children will be waiting for us, and where we'll introduce the very quiet bundle of joy to them. There isn't a doubt in my mind the twins will be over the moon in love with our-yet-to-be named little boy. It's Quinn who I worry about the most.

He's always been our only son, the only brother. I can't imagine at his age what he's going to think of this new little guy. I lean toward the middle of the console, wishing I could see the baby or had sat in the back with him. I almost did until Harrison told me to let him sleep. He was right. Had I sat back there, I would've touched his cheeks, lips, and adjusted the blanket covering him, which would've surely woken him.

"We're almost there," Harrison says. I glance out the front and notice very little traffic heading toward the airport.

"You'd think more people would be traveling right now."

"Probably next week, a little closer to Christmas."

He reminds me that I need to text Jenna. I pull out my phone and ask her if the packages arrived. She responds with a picture of her holding a coffee mug with the fireplace in the background.

"What is it?" Harrison asks.

"Oh, nothing. Jenna's sitting by the fire and enjoying a cup of coffee."

Harrison laughs. "I'm willing to bet there's some Bailey's in there, and she probably loves the peace and quiet."

"You're probably right. How do you think Eden is doing on the slopes?"

"Knowing her, she's probably a natural."

"Once again, you're probably right."

Harrison signals to turn into the parking lot of the hotel, and my stomach seizes. He must sense my anxiety building because he tells me everything will be fine. After he parks, he pulls out his phone and tells the kids to all meet in Peyton's room, that we'll be there in a moment.

"What if they're mad?"

"They won't be," he says, although I don't find his words reassuring, just pointed.

Harrison gets out first and must-see my hesitation because he has my door open and is unbuckling my seatbelt so he can pull me into his arms. When he releases me, his hand cups my cheek, and he looks into my eyes. "We have the most amazing kids we could ever ask for. I think, if anything, they'll be concerned for us and the lack of sleep we're going to get for a few months and the legal battle we'll face when we go to adopt him. I know they'll be supportive and will fall completely in love with him." He nods toward the back. "I also know, they're expecting us, and they know something is up. If we don't get up there soon, one of them is bound to come looking for us."

"I'm about to say you're right, but I have a feeling you already know this," I quip.

Harrison kisses my forehead, and I feel his lips forming into a smile. When he pulls away, the grin is from ear to ear. "As I've said many, many times over the years, I plug into greatness every night." He winks at his sexual innuendo and leaves me sitting there. I'm stunned by his comment and shouldn't be. I'm used to the things he says, inappropriate or not.

He opens the back door and grabs the car seat from the base, and carries it effortlessly as we head into the hotel. After a quick elevator ride, we're standing outside Peyton's room. Before either of us knock, Harrison sets the carrier down on the floor, out of sight from the door.

"Do you trust me?"

"Of course," I tell him. "With my life."

He knocks, and the door swings open. Peyton stands there, with her long chestnut hair cascading down her back, wearing a T-shirt that reads, "My Husband Goes Deep." I blush at the wording, and while Harrison may not be her biological father, their humor is one and the same.

"You're being weird. What's going on?" she says before we have a chance to hug her or even say hi.

"Your mom and I have something to show you, but I need for the four of you to turn around, no peeking."

Peyton sighs dramatically and then says, "Okay, you heard the man. Turn around."

Elle and Quinn stand and turn around. We wait for Peyton to move closer to her siblings before working as a team to get the baby out of his carrier. With him in my arms and with Harrison standing next to me, we enter the room and stand behind our children.

"Merry Christmas," Harrison says.

The three of them turn around. After this moment, I'm not going to remember who's expression I looked at first, but I'm going to remember that it was Peyton who stepped forward.

"Mom, what's going on?" she asks as her hands hover over the bundle in my arms.

"This little guy needed a family, and we just happen to have the perfect one," Harrison says as he touches the baby's cheek, which lifts.

"Wait, he's ours?" Elle asks.

"For right now," I tell them. "We intend to adopt him."

"Whoa," Quinn says as he comes closer. "He's tiny."

I nod. "He's a safe haven baby. I've been holding him at the hospital since he came in."

"Are you sure you guys want to do this all over again?" Elle asks. "You're going to be grandparents soon."

My eyes shoot to Elle's. "Are you pregnant?"

"What? No!" she blanches.

"Me neither," Nola blurts out.

"Or me," says Peyton.

"What's his name?" Quinn asks.

"Well, that's where you guys come in. We wanted to decide as a family." Harrison motions for everyone to sit and gather around the small table in the room. He tells the two names we decided on, Oliver and Ezra. "Write your choice on a piece of paper, fold it, and hand it to me." Harrison rips up a sheet of paper from the tablet on the table and hands each of us a piece. We only have one pen, so he hands it to me first, and I pass it on to Elle. When we're all done, Harrison has a small pile in front of him.

"Okay," he starts. "We have a vote for Oliver."

I look down at the baby and bounce him a little.

"Next one is for Oliver. And the next. And we have one for Ezra. Again, for Oliver. And the final one is for Ezra." Harrison looks at me and smiles. "Looks like your name is going to be Oliver Powell-James, little buddy."

"Ollie for short," Elle says.

"Ollie . . . I like it," I add. "Welcome to your family, Ollie."

We spend the next hour or so passing Oliver around and posing for our first family photo. The girls are bummed they can't post our picture on social media but understand the rules. When it's time to leave, Quinn is the one who picks up Ollie's carrier.

"Your dad can carry him," I say as I run my fingers over his shaggy hair.

"I know, but I want to."

"Are you okay with all of this?"

He nods and pulls me into a one-armed hug. "I think this is amazing. This little guy has no idea how lucky he is. The girls and I had the best life growing up, and Oliver is going to be so loved."

"You're going to the best big brother, Quinn. And when the time is right, the best father."

Quinn chuckles and rolls his eyes. "Do we have Ollie because you're ready to be a grandma?" His eyebrow goes up in question.

I shake my head. "Not at all. From the moment I held him and heard his story, I knew he was put in my life for a reason. Even if Nola, Elle, and Peyton come to me tomorrow and say they're having babies, that would just make life even much better."

"Okay, just wanted to check." He winks at me, reminding me of his father. If Oliver turns out to be like my James men, his future spouse will be very lucky.

By the time we get to the hangar, Oliver is awake, and the girls are cooing up a storm. I'm almost jealous that I have to share him with anyone. I was the same when the twins were born. My parents and in-laws wanted them all the time, and I never wanted to give them up. Of course, that changed when the cuteness of having newborns wore off, and I longed for a five-minute nap that didn't include puke on my shirt or a pail of dirty diapers that needed to go out. I had Mason though, and as soon as he came home from work, he took his dad duty to the next level, which allowed me to be human for a bit. I'm confident Harrison is going to be the same type of dad to Oliver. I also have a feeling that Elle and Quinn will be over a lot. Maybe even Nola.

Harrison, Quinn, and the ground crew get the plane loaded, and by the time I've given up supervising my guys, I find that the twins and Nola have Oliver out of his carrier and are taking turns holding him. I don't know how long I stand there, watching them. I have no doubt they'll make amazing mothers when the time is right for them.

When Harrison's arms slip around my waist, I lean into his chest. "Look at them."

"I'm looking."

Quinn passes by us and heads to his sisters and the love of his life. The only one missing from the picture is Noah. Suddenly, my hand flies to my mouth in disbelief.

"What's wrong?"

Slowly, I shake my head as hurt and anger pools within. "I completely forgot about Ajay in all of this. He should be here. My grandbabies should be here to meet their . . . well calling Oliver their uncle just seems weird to me."

Harrison holds me tighter. "They went to North Carolina for the holidays, but I'll text him and let him know that we're somewhat close if he and Jamie want to come up after Christmas with the kids."

"I'll call Jamie later. I want to talk to Evelyn and let her know that Grandma and Grandpa didn't forget about her and James."

"I'm sure she knows." Harrison takes my hand and leads me farther into the plane. The pilot speaks over the intercom and tells us we're about to start our journey. I'm tempted to ask the girls to hand Oliver over to me, but I know my request will fall on deaf ears. At this point, I'll be lucky if I get to hold my son again until we're back in California. Something tells me Oliver is going to win over every female member of our family, the guys as well.

11

HARRISON

In all my life, I never thought I'd fly across the United States with a newborn. When Quinn was born, the band traveled via charter bus. Being on tour with an infant was never ideal, but I always thought it was better than being on a plane where the air pressure could hurt Quinn's ears. When he was fussy, I'd walk around the bus with him. Again, not ideal, but it worked. Also, having JD and Liam on board helped. We took turns holding him, much like the way the twins, Nola and Quinn, are doing now with Oliver. I swear, every time I look over, Oliver is resting in someone else's arms, and Katelyn is intently focused on the group. I have a feeling she wants the baby back in her arms, and honestly, I don't blame her. I'd like to hold him too. I want to bond, even though, as foster parents, we shouldn't. Oliver's placement with us could be temporary. His mother or father could come back and say they want him, and we'd have to let him go. I've been down this road before with Quinn, and was so thankful when Alicia gave up her rights.

Although, that really never stopped her from meddling in my life or trying to ruin Quinn's. The thing is, knowing what I know—what Katelyn and I know—we're willing to do it all over again to give Oliver a chance at a good life.

I must've lost track of time or stopped paying attention to everything around me but my children because when our pilot tells us, we're starting our descent, I'm surprised by how quicky the flight went. And at some point, Katelyn had curled up with a throw blanket and fell asleep. Before the pilot reminds us to remain seated, I get up and make sure everyone has buckled up. It's really a ploy to check on Oliver, even though I know he's in good hands. I find him snuggled in his seat, asleep. But it's his hands that bring a smile to my face. Both Peyton and Elle are holding onto his tiny little hands. This little boy has no idea how loved he is right now.

"You guys good?" I whisper to Quinn and Nola. She has her head on his shoulder, and looks up and nods at me. When I make it back to Katelyn, I slide in behind her and kiss her lightly on the space between her shoulder and neck. She hums in delight. "We're about to land."

Katelyn sits upright, stretches, and reaches for her seat belt. "Where's Oliver?"

"He's with the twins. It's a picture-perfect moment. They're all holding hands."

In a flash, Katelyn throws the blanket off her lap, releases the lap belt, and makes her way to where the twins are seated. I never take my eyes off her and know I did the right thing by telling her when I see her hand cover her mouth. She comes back with me with tears in her eyes. "They're perfect."

I nod and wait for her to sit down next to me. "And

Quinn is just across from them. It's like old times when they were younger, and we used to travel. The three of them have always been inseparable. They have this entire plane to spread out, and they're together."

"We must've done something right," Katelyn says. She has no idea how right she is.

"I know I did." I push her hair behind her ear and lean in to kiss her. "Meeting you on Christmas was the best thing to ever happen to me." Our lips finally touch. I know she'll never tell me the same thing, and I'm okay with it. Katelyn had a life before me, one that she thought she'd have until the day she died, and I will never ask her or the girls to forget about Mason. It would be unfair of me. I knew what I was getting into when I pursued Katelyn.

The plane touches down, and even though the landing is as smooth as it can for December in Vermont, we still jostle around a bit. Oliver starts to cry, and Katelyn is out of her seat before the pilot gives us the okay to move about the cabin. I have a feeling she and her daughters will fight over who gets to soothe Oliver's tears.

When we're finally in the hangar, I stand and go meet the pilot, thanking him for getting us here safely, and we talk about what the rest of the month entails. By the time I've finished with the pilot, all our belongings are loaded into the back of the two SUVs I rented. The plan is for Quinn to drive one while I drive the other. The problem I didn't foresee is unfolding right in front of my eyes—who will ride with Oliver. The twins want to ride with us, which is fine. But I know Katelyn would like to sit in the back seat with the baby. And then there's Nola, who Elle is trying to convince to ride with her and Peyton.

I glance over at Quinn, who is leaning against the car, tapping his foot. Is he frustrated or humored by everything that is going on? He's probably a little bit of both, as I am. I'd like to get on the road. According to the research I did, there's a saying in Vermont that if you don't like the weather, wait five minutes, and it'll change. I also learned about snow squalls and how deadly they can be, especially at night. They sound like something I don't want to get caught in.

"Ladies, the loves of us three James men's lives," I say to get all their attention. "We need to get on the road. I'd really like to get to the lodge sooner rather than later, and it's already getting dark out."

"Maybe we should rent a hotel for the night," Katelyn suggests. "This way, we can drive in the daylight and not worry about the backroads."

While I like the thought, I am also looking forward to relaxing in the hot tub and chilling with JD, Liam, and a few cold ones.

"I'd rather leave now while the weather is clear," Quinn says. "According to the app, it's going to snow tomorrow, and I've heard this place can be unpredictable with snowfall."

"Weather is unpredictable," Elle says.

"Yes, but Vermont is notorious for saying they're getting a blizzard, and they get a flurry or two, or the weatherman tells everyone the storm is going to miss them, and they wake up to thirty inches. I'm just saying, I'd rather head toward the mountain now, knowing it's not snowing instead of waiting to see what is going to happen in the morning," Quinn rebuts his sister.

"I agree with Quinn," Katelyn concedes. "He's right. We should get going."

Music to my ears. "Now, who is going to ride with Oliver?"

Many hands go up, but it's Elle who relents. "I'll go with Quinn and Nola," she says just before she gives Oliver one last look. "He is really cute," she tells all of us. I happen to agree and wish I could take all the credit for his looks, but the only one I'll ever be able to claim is Quinn.

We finally pile into the cars, and I decide to follow Quinn. He's much more versed in the matters of navigation and technology. Plus, his co-pilot will help him. Mine is making baby noises in the back seat and trying to convince our daughter that she needs a baby of her own.

IT'S pitch black by the time we arrive at the lodge, although you would never know it by the well-lit parking lot and trails. The people skiing at night look like tiny specs cruising down the mountain, and if you look closely and focus, you can see snow kicking up from their skis. What surprises me the most is the location of the house. When I was told it was at the base of the lodge, I didn't think Katelyn meant it in the literal sense. I was wrong. If I had to give directions to this place, I'd say it's in the parking lot. In fact, there are five designated parking spots just for the house itself.

No sooner do I have the car in park does the front door fly open. The squeals are ear piercing as Liam comes running toward me with his arms out. As soon as he reaches me, he's wrapped me in his arms. The only thing missing is his legs hitched over my hips.

"What are you doing?" I squeeze out through panted

breaths. If I didn't know any better, I'd think he's trying to suffocate me.

"I've missed you," he says. It's true we haven't seen each other much. I've hinted that he should move back to Los Angeles, but he won't unless it's something Josie suggests. I respect that as his friend. As his bandmate, I feel like 4225 West has been pushed aside because of the member's distance. I know we've been around for over twenty years, but many bands are still making music and selling out venues. That could still be us.

"I've missed you too," I tell him. I'm being honest. I do miss being around him all the time. "Listen, we sort of have a surprise for everyone. Mind going in and making sure everyone is gathered in the living room or something?"

"What's going on?"

I grip his shoulder and shake my head. "Inside. Even the infamous Liam Page has to wait for the news."

Liam nods and heads back inside after saying hi to everyone. I tell Quinn that we'll come back for the luggage after we've had a chance to introduce the newest member of our family to everyone, and Elle tells us how we're going to walk into the house. I'm going in first, followed by Quinn and Nola, with the twins next, and finally Katelyn and Oliver. Truthfully, I want to be with Katelyn, but sometimes there is no use in arguing with Elle. She's headstrong and very set in her ways.

As instructed, we fall in line and head into the house. As much as I want to look around and take everything in, it'll have to wait until later. Right now, I have far more important things to do, like introduce my son to my best friends. Quinn and Nola follow me in and stand off to the side.

"What's going?" Josie asks.

"We have something to tell everyone," I say as the twins walk in.

"Oh my god, which one of you is pregnant?" Josie blurts out.

"Why? Why must one of us be pregnant?" Elle asks.

"It's not me," Nola chimes in.

"Nor me," Peyton says. "You would already know if I was that's for sure."

Josie stands, as does Jenna. "Okay, you need to . . ." Josie's words are cut off when Katelyn comes into view with the car carrier. "I know I haven't seen you in a couple of months, but surely you would've told me if you were pregnant."

Jenna's mouth opens as if she's going to say something and then closes it again. I look at Liam, who appears thoroughly confused, his brows knitted together. It's JD who walks in behind Katelyn, none the wiser that the Jameses are trying to make a grand entrance. "Whoa, who's bub is this?"

"He's ours," Katelyn says.

"What?" Liam, Josie, Jenna, and JD say in unison.

"Everyone, I'd like for you to meet Oliver James. Well, he will be a James after we can file for adoption."

Katelyn takes our son from his carrier and shows him to his family. There are many oohs and aahs and still some confused looks, mostly from JD and Liam. I go to them and say, "I'll tell you guys later over a game of pool or something."

"Are you happy?" Liam asks.

I think about his question for a minute and try not to focus on Katelyn and the excitement she's showing. The smile forms before I start to nod. "I am," I tell my friends and son, who has joined us. "Once you hold him, you'll see why."

"It's like magic," Quinn adds. "He's a Christmas miracle."

12

JENNA

Poor little Oliver is passed from person to person, with each of us making the most ridiculous faces at him. He's a trooper though, and barely fusses. It's like we're in an assembly line, each waiting a turn to hold him. When he finally gets to me—which seems like ages from when Katelyn walked in with him—my heart simultaneously beats with happiness for my friend and breaks for myself. For years, Jimmy and I tried to have another child, but it just wasn't in the cards for us. We went to doctors, specialists and they all said the same thing: there isn't anything wrong, keep trying. We thought about IVF, but I pushed it aside, thinking that when my body was ready for another child, it would happen. Now, I fear it's too late but seeing Katelyn come in with this bundle of joy gives me hope. Maybe Jimmy and I can explore adoption as he suggested in the past. However, I'm not sure how Eden would feel. I'd love to think her reaction would be the same as Elle, Peyton, and Quinn's was, but being an only child is different.

I'm not sure how long I get to hold Oliver, but grabby

hands, also known as my husband, takes him from me and starts speaking cockney to him. I roll my eyes, and I think a few others do as well, except for the guys. Liam and Harrison are going gaga over the baby, right along with Jimmy.

Katelyn comes back into the room and takes the empty spot next to me on the sofa. She hands me a glass of wine and sets another one down for Josie, who comes back into the living room with a bowl of chips and salsa. Jimmy, Eden, and I were the first to arrive and had the house to ourselves for the first day. Well, I should say, I had the house to myself because Eden and Jimmy hit the slopes first thing when we arrived and again this morning. It seems snowboarding is natural for Eden, and she can't get enough of some pipe or something. The lingo is confusing, but I try to keep up with what she's telling me.

Josie sits with a sigh and rests her head on the back of the couch. "This house—"

"It's amazing," I tell her. "The pool, or rather the oasis, is beyond words. As soon as Jimmy and Eden left this morning, I floated around that thing for over an hour. I think the best part is the glass ceiling. Watching the snowfall is magical."

"How did you find this place?" Katelyn asks.

"Internet," Josie says. "I just started searching for houses to fit our family size. I found a bunch, and then I narrowed it down to where I thought we'd like to visit. Vermont seemed like a fun wintery getaway. Plus, the questionable cell service is nice. I want everyone to unplug and relax while we're here."

"I, for one, am happy Eden put her phone away. I think this is good for her and Jimmy. It's something differ-ent. She focuses so much on surfing, which I know it's too late to do anything about it. I read this article the other day about kids who specialize in one sport, which got me thinking. She never really tried anything other than surfing."

"No thanks to Quinn," Katelyn says with a laugh. "Does she still have a crush on him?"

I nod. "I think she was rather put off that Nola came. I think Eden looked forward to monopolizing his time."

"Quinn will still spend time with her. Nola is not a fan of the snow or the wintry weather. She'll likely stay inside with us," Katelyn tells us. "In fact, I think this might be the first time she's spent any considerable amount of time in it."

"And me," Peyton says as she comes into the room. Elle and Nola follow her. The three of them are carrying a glass of wine.

"Who stocked the liquor?" Elle asks.

"I did," Josie says. "Is there enough? Do I need to order more?"

Elle shakes her head and holds up her glass. "I'm curious about this wine. It's delicious."

There's a look of relief on Josie's face. "Oh, thank god. For a minute, I thought you were going to tell me it sucked or something."

"Not at all," Elle replies. "I'd like to visit the winery before we leave. Do you think they're open?"

"Yes, I looked at their websites before we came and wrote everything down. They have tastings and are open through the holidays. I'd love to go with you if you want the company."

"I'd love that, Aunt Josie."

"I'm in," adds Nola. "That's if I'm invited."

Elle looks at her oddly. "As if we'd leave you behind." She turns and looks at her sister. "You?"

Peyton shrugs. It makes me wonder if it's because Noah will be here soon or if she's still suffering some PTSD from her accident.

Elle groans. "Seriously? Because of Noah?"

Peyton looks sharply at her sister. "He can't ski when he's here, so if we all take off for a girl's day, he's left alone unless one of the guys stays behind. So, excuse me if I decide to stay back with my husband."

Just then, the door opens, and all heads turn toward whoever walked in. The chattering voices of Betty Paige and an unfamiliar voice fill the air. I glance at Josie, who shrugs. "I forgot to mention we have a visitor."

"Mack!" Peyton exclaims as she stands and goes to him. She pulls Mack into her arms. "What are you doing here?"

Mack glances at Josie, who says, "I'll fill them in. Why don't you and Paige get ready? We'll go into town and pick up some pizzas." Mack nods and heads down one of the hallways. Once he's out of sight, Josie takes a long sip of her wine and starts talking. "Nick and Aubrey are getting a divorce. She's taking Amelia back to South Africa, and Mack is staying in Beaumont. We originally invited Mack to come after Christmas, but Nick asked Liam if we could bring Mack with us now."

"Does Noah know?" Peyton asks.

Josie shakes her head. "I don't think so. I doubt Nick confided in Noah that his marriage is falling apart."

"No, but we would've taken Mack," Peyton adds.

Josie smiles. "That's very sweet of you, but we both know that's not feasible. Mack's doing very well in school and excelling in his sports. Nick doesn't want Mack to give that up. As long as Mack is in Beaumont, Liam and I will make sure he's taken care of."

"Wait, can you go back to the Liam part?" Katelyn asks.

Josie laughs and rolls her eyes. "It seems Nick found Liam at the water tower a few nights back and told him everything. He asked for our help, and Liam agreed."

"Whoa," Katelyn says.

"I know," Josie adds. "I don't think they're besties just yet, but maybe." She laughs. We all know Liam and Nick Ashford will never be best friends. Cordial, yes. But anything else is pushing it.

"I think I'm in shock," I say. "Liam has allowed his daughter's crush to come on holiday with her?"

"He's a changed man." Josie laughs. "Actually, it took some prodding at first. Like I said, Mack was going to join us after Christmas, which would give him a day or two with Noah. But then Nick . . . well you know the rest. I do think Liam put the fear of God into the boy though, but we'll still keep our eyes on them."

"Right because we were . . ." Katelyn stops talking and looks at her girls. She smiles sheepishly and then turns back to her glass of wine.

"Mom, seriously?" Peyton says.

"Please tell us it was our father, and you weren't some —ouch," Elle looks at her sister in horror. "I can't believe you just hit me."

"So, what if Mom had a couple of boyfriends."

"I just don't want to hear about her sexcapades when she was a teen." Elle shudders, and we all laugh.

"What's going on in here?" Harrison asks as he enters the room, cradling Oliver. I reach for him, hoping Katelyn won't be angry that I want to hold him again.

Harrison sets him into my arms, and I sigh with happiness.

"Does he have a nickname or anything?"

"Ollie," Katelyn says. "Harrison and I settled on two names, and then as a family, we voted."

"What was the other name?" Josie asks from behind me. She's moved so she can look at the sleeping bundle in my arms.

"Ezra."

"He looks like an Ollie to me," Peyton says. "And Oliver fits when you say all our names together."

"Does he have a middle name?" I ask.

Katelyn shakes her head. "Oliver Powell-James is already a mouthful. No need to add any more. But he won't officially be Oliver until the adoption. Right now, the state refers to him as Baby John Doe, but Harrison wanted to make sure we called him something else because Jimmy—"

"Do not tell Jimmy the baby has his initials. You'll never hear the end of it," I tell Katelyn.

"Exactly what Harrison said."

Betty Paige and Mack walk into the room. I look for signs they were making out but see nothing. Mack sits on the floor in front of Peyton, and they start talking quietly. You can clearly see the adoration they have for each other. Paige sits next to Josie and eyes me warily.

"Um, Aunt Jenna, what's in your arms?"

"A baby," I tell her as I hold him up for her to see. Her eyes go wide.

"Who had a baby?"

"Well, I kind of did," Katelyn says. "We are fostering until we can adopt him."

Paige moves closer to me and gets a better look at Oliver. "What's his name?"

"Oliver," I tell her.

"Where's his mom?"

"She can't take care of him, so we're going to," Katelyn answers. I'm not sure how you explain to a teenager that someone abandoned their baby. I know the safe haven laws don't call it abandonment, but it still feels that way to me, especially when I've wanted another baby for so long.

"It's sad that his mom left him," Mack chimes in. "But it's good that you have him, Miss Katelyn. He's a lucky boy." It makes me wonder if his statement is some sort of reflection or jab at his mom for wanting to move out of the country.

"We're the lucky ones," Katelyn replies.

The door opens again, and this time it's Eden. It takes her a few minutes to get her gear off, but she's in shock when she comes into the room until Paige fills her in. Within an instant of learning that the baby I'm holding is not staying with us, she's next to me, making the most adorable sounds at Oliver.

"Peyton, don't you want one?" her sister asks.

All eyes are on Peyton while we wait for the answer. I know everyone is excited for her and Noah to start a family, but I also respect why they haven't. Peyton is young and just starting her career. I'm sure she wants to make a name for herself with the Pioneers before she goes out on maternity leave. Unlike Noah's job, she doesn't get an off-season because she works with management when it comes time to recruit. From what Katelyn has told me, Peyton is always watching game film of college kids, looking to see who might bring new life or fill a void in the team. Her job isn't to just break down Noah's game, but the whole team and make them better.

"We do when the time is right," she says to everyone, mostly eyeing her mother and sister.

"Until then," Josie says, "You can play with this cute little boy." She reaches for him, and I reluctantly hand him over. I know I have to share, but I don't want to. It's selfish, I know. Maybe it is time for Jimmy and me to explore adoption.

13

JIMMY

Leave it to Harrison to change the dynamic of our lives. I don't blame my mate for doing what his missus wants, to be honest I'd move heaven and earth to give Jenna everything she wanted, but a baby is another story. For whatever reason, we couldn't have a second child. We tried a lot, which honestly is the best part, but there were a few miscarriages, a lot of tests, and a load of doctors saying there's nothing wrong with either of us. Their answer was IVF, which basically means they take my swimmers in a cup and do what they have to do with them. But for Jenna, those drugs would've taken a toll on her both emotionally and physically. Even so, I would've held her hand, held her hair back when she was throwing up and given her the jabs. In the end, she decided not to go through with it. Jenna has always told me she's happy with our life, just the three of us, but watching her tonight, I know she's not being completely truthful with me.

My mates and I are hanging out in the kitchen with a

clear view of the ladies as they go completely gaga over the newest member of our family. The house Josie rented for us is massive and is an open plan, which I'm not a fan of because I like walls. Walls mean I can hang our gold and platinum records, as well as our awards. They mean I can show off all the women in my life by displaying their photos, artwork, and the kindergarten finger painting Eden did for me. It's of our tour bus, with her standing in front, holding my hand. At least, that's what she told me when she gave it to me before we left on tour years ago. Still, this house rivals anything I've seen. Jenna kept saying there was a hot tub, but that's an understatement. There's an indoor pool with a grotto and a way to go outside and enjoy the freshly falling snow with your missus. It's romantic as hell, but more importantly, each of the bedrooms are far away from each other, so when the mood strikes, and, let's be honest, it's going to strike, we'll all have privacy.

Eden, Betty Paige, and Mack walk into the kitchen. They're raiding the fridge and talking with each other, not caring that their fathers are all within hearing distance of them. I eye them for a minute, amused by the fact that Mack is here. He's my focus right now and how he moves around Paige. Liam must be shitting his pants right about now.

"I don't get it," I say as soon as the kids leave. "Aren't you worried about Mack and Paige?"

Liam pales and tips the can of beer he has in his hand. It's from a local brewer called 14th Star Brewing Co. and was recommended by the bartender at the lodge. He hooked me on their beer, Valor, and I went out earlier today and bought as much as I could of all their products.

What I really like about them, aside from the taste, is that two friends who served in the war started the company after one came up with the idea on the battlefield.

"What's that?" Liam asks, even though I suspect he knows what I'm talking about.

"Mack." Harrison clears his throat and looks at Liam while I lean forward. "Spill."

Liam groans, takes a long drink from the can, and sets it back down onto the table. "You know, sometimes I wish I had put my foot down and told Ashford to take a hike. But I know deep down, if I had, I would've lost Noah. And likely Josie because we would've fought about Nick and Noah being in each other's lives. Had Sam . . ." Liam trails off. The bane of our lives, well mostly Liam and Harrison's, was Sam, our former manager. I never really gave her the time of day, other than needing a job from her. She mostly stayed out of my life and only meddled when Chelsea and I broke up. Even though Sam died years ago, it seems my mates are still dealing with her bullshit. Liam stands and goes to the fridge. He comes back with six more beers and hands two to each of us. We all open them at the same time and take a drink.

"The other night, I'm at the water tower, doing my thing."

"You mean you had your own pity party?" Harrison asks. He's smiling, but Liam isn't. We all know Liam wishes we still lived in Beaumont with him and have begged him to move back to Los Angeles. Harrison and I get it. His life is there, but he's built himself a nice life in L.A. too, and I know Katelyn and Jenna would be ecstatic to have Josie there.

"Yeah, something like that," Liam says. "Anyway,

Ashford shows up. Earlier, Paige had asked us if Mack could come with us on this trip. I was adamant the kid stays home with his parents but conceded that he could come the day after Christmas and stay with us until we went back. When Ashford showed up, I thought he was there to discuss Mack and Paige." Liam takes another sip and pauses before finishing. "Nick and Aubrey are getting divorced, and she's taking Amelia to South Africa to live. Mack is staying in Beaumont."

"Whoa," Harrison says.

Liam nods. "I wasn't expecting him to ask me to keep his son over the holidays."

"Why did you?" I ask.

"Because of Noah. I know for some it might be hard to justify why I'd let some hormonal teen stay in my house, especially when my daughter has a massive crush on him, but the truth is, Noah would want me to. He thinks of Nick as a father, and I can't change that, which means he thinks of Mack as a brother. I'm not going to let Mack suffer because his parents have hit a rough patch. Noah would never forgive me."

"I'm not sure I'd be able to do it. Let some bloke sleep in a room next to my daughter, especially one she has eyes for," I say.

Liam smirks. "I don't think I've slept since Mack arrived at the house the other night. He's broken though. He knows what's going on with his parents. His sister is leaving. He's going to need some constant in his life, and I think Josie and I can provide that for the time being. It'll be a good thing for Mack when Noah arrives."

"Aren't you afraid of what might happen?" I nod toward the room where everyone is, not knowing if the kids are in there or not.

Liam shakes his head slowly. "No, I'm not. Mack knows not to disrespect my rules."

"You're very trusting, my friend." Harrison squeezes Liam's shoulder.

"So are you," Liam laughs. "Lest I remind you about my son and your daughter."

Harrison stands and picks up his full can of beer. He points at Liam with his other hand. "True love, man. True love," he says with a pretend sob.

Liam and I follow Harrison into the other room. The ladies are still in awe over Ollie, which I get. Thankfully, Jenna's arms are empty. I'd hate to take time away from her and the baby. "Wanna head to the pool?" Jenna nods and reaches for my hand to help her up.

"Where are you going?" Katelyn asks.

"To the pool? You should come with us," I say.

"You know, you guys haven't even seen the house. Come on, let me show you around before I take the kids to pick up the pizzas," Josie says as she stands.

Liam puts his beer down on the coffee table and tells Harrison he and Mack will get their things from the cars so everyone can tour the house. "Mack," he yells, and within seconds the boy appears.

"Yes, sir?"

"Do you want to help me get the Jameses' luggage from their cars while Josie shows them around the house?"

I notice that Liam asks Mack to help and doesn't tell him he has to. To me, Liam is showing Mack the respect he's demanding in return.

"Of course," Mack says straight away. There isn't any hesitation in his answer. In fact, he's already putting his coat on.

"I'll help," I add, even though I'd rather get half-naked with my wife. Helping to unload the cars is the right thing to do though. After I get bundled up because it's bloody well freezing outside, we head out. I'm grateful for snow-blowers, deep shovels, and plows for clearing as much of the snow away as possible. Those tools make it so much easier to walk around, although you still have to watch for ice. I already slipped on some earlier and about fell flat on my arse. Jenna laughed and said my arms looked like windmills. I found none of it funny.

I can easily say this, the Jameses pack way too much stuff. It takes Mack and me two trips to bring everything into the house. After the first load, Liam complained of a broken fingernail or some stupid shit like that and used it as an excuse to seek medical attention. I should've known he'd flake out.

"What's it like to live with Liam?" I ask Mack as we shed our winter gear.

"Well, sir," he says. "It's only been a few days."

"I'm Jimmy. The guys call me JD. You can call me either, I don't mind, but you don't have to call me sir. Does Liam make you call him that?"

Mack shakes his head. "No, si . . . JD. He's told me before I can call him Liam, but my parents want me to call him Mr. Westbury. I think that's odd though because Noah's my brother and Liam's his dad, so I call him sir."

"You must be excited to see Noah tomorrow?"

Mack nods. "He can't ski or snowboard though. Quinn said he'd go with me."

"I'll go too," I tell him. "Turns out I quite like snow-boarding."

"It's fun," Mack says. He quiets as soon as Betty Paige enters the foyer. There is no mistaking the chemistry between them. If Liam doesn't keep a watchful eye on these two, he's going to become a grandpa sooner than he's expecting. "Hey." Mack's voice has completely changed to a soft tone.

"Everyone's going swimming," Paige says as she points towards the pool. "Do you want to go?"

Mack doesn't say anything for a bit but finally nods. It's hard for me to say, but I think the poor guy looked Paige up and down before he could find the right words to reply. Yep, Liam is in for a world of trouble.

"Paige, give Mack and me a few, and we'll meet you all at the pool."

She smiles and walks away. I place my hand on Mack's shoulder and give him a fair shake. "Don't even think about it."

"What?" he asks with wide, startled eyes.

"Her. You. Doing things to make Liam kill you."

Mack hangs his head. "I'm thankful to be here, but she's hard to be around sometimes."

"It's called hormones. You've got to get a control on them because the result of acting on them before you're ready could end very badly."

"Yeah, I told Mr. Westbury I'd respect his rules, and I will. She," he pauses and points. "Makes it very hard."

I make a mental note to say something to Jenna in the hope she'll say something to Josie about the temptations of having both these kids living in their house. Maybe Josie will tell Paige she needs to take it down a notch or two before these teens find themselves in a situation they can't get out of.

With my hand still on his shoulder, I signal for him to follow me. When we get to his room, I leave him there but before I go, I tell him if he needs to talk, I'd be happy to lend an ear and offer some advice. I leave out the part where I'm probably the last bloke he should ask for advice, especially considering I was having sex, drinking, and partying at his age. As a father of a teenager though, I'm pretty sure I can offer words of wisdom. At least, I hope I can.

14

———

JOSIE

When I wake, my hand reaches for Liam, only to remember he and most of the crew decided to rent snowmobiles the day before and planned to leave early in the morning. Elle found a brochure for a diner, out in the middle of nowhere and only accessible by sled, dubbed the best breakfast in New England. She jokingly suggested they go, and the guys jumped on the idea. With Noah having to stay back, I decided I would stay with him. Besides, sometimes a mom just needs a little time with her baby boy.

I find Noah sitting in one of the oversized chairs with a mug of coffee resting on the table next to him. The fire is roaring, emitting so much heat we can easily walk around in pajama shorts or a pair of thin flannel pants. He doesn't hear me walking behind him, which tells me he's deep in thought. The closer I get to him I can see why. He's holding Ollie, who is awake and looking wide-eyed at Noah.

"Good morning." I ruffle his hair, much like I've done his entire life. "I see you found a friend."

"Morning," he says. "I woke up with Peyton and found Katelyn out here. She looked like she wanted to go with everyone, so I volunteered us to watch Oliver. I hope you don't mind."

"I don't mind." I smile softly at my son and then head into the kitchen to pour myself a cup of coffee and grab a muffin. "Do you want a muffin?" I holler out to Noah.

"Blueberry if there is one."

I take two and set them each onto their own plate and into the microwave for thirty seconds. Once they're done, I add a bit of butter, grab forks, and carry the small plates with one hand and my coffee in the other.

"I see all those years as a waitress are paying off," he says as I head toward him. He reaches for a plate and fork and thanks me.

"You're funny." I sit down and curl my legs up underneath me and start picking at my breakfast. "I'm surprised Peyton went this morning."

"It wasn't without a lot of urging, that's for sure."

"Is everything okay?" For a while, I've had sinking suspicion that something is going on. I don't want to prod into my son's life, but I also don't want him to suffer in silence.

"It's not what you think." Noah adjusts a sleeping Oliver so that he can eat his muffin. I offer to take the baby, but Noah refuses. "Peyton and I are solid, and there isn't anything wrong outside of our marriage or with us working together, although the guys do like to give me shit because my wife gets paid to tell me when I suck."

"I'm sure she doesn't use those words."

Noah laughs. "No, she doesn't. Even when Peyton's delivering bad news, she does it in such a positive way we don't realize she's telling us we're horrible," Noah pauses and takes a bite of his food and washes it down with coffee. "I'm on edge, and maybe she is too, because of me, due to some things going on with the guys. Julius's wife wants a divorce and plans to take the kids back to Los Angeles, and Alex and his girlfriend broke up, which is messing with his head a bit."

"You can't shoulder everyone's burden," I tell him. "Your dad used to do that. He'd worry about Harrison or Jimmy, and then he'd start to second-guess himself. He feels like their happiness is his responsibility."

"Yeah, I get it. Speaking of—" Noah looks at with his eyebrow cocked. "Nick and Aubrey?"

I nod slowly. "I didn't see that one coming. Did you?"

"Definitely not. A little heads up would've been nice though. When I came down the escalator at the airport, I saw Peyton and then Mack. He was in my arms, crying before I could even move out of the way from the people behind me."

"Nick wanted to tell you. It must've slipped his mind."

"So, what's the story? Mack only said that his mom is leaving."

"Your dad knows more than I do, but the gist is, Aubrey wants to go back to South Africa and wants to take the kids but agreed to let Mack stay in Beaumont."

"Wow," Noah says with a shake of his head. "And then this guy." He looks down at Ollie and smiles. "Peyton talked a mile a minute on the drive back on how excited she was for her parents and how it all seemed so perfect to welcome him into the family."

I watch my son with Oliver for a long moment and wonder if I should ask him about what's on my mind. Noah glances up and looks at me oddly.

"What?" he asks.

I shrug. "Just wondering."

He shakes his head slowly. "I know it's on your mind and Katelyn's too, and it's not that we don't want to have children. We do. We're not careful at all, but it just hasn't happened. If it does, great. If not . . . well, I don't know. We haven't really explored other options, but the doctors have warned us that Peyton may not be able to get pregnant because of the accident. She has a considerable amount of scarring."

My hand covers my mouth. I should've known there might be issues from the car accident. I think deep down I had hoped that things would've just been back to normal for Peyton over time. I didn't want to think she and Noah wouldn't be able to have children.

"Well," I start to say before I become choked up. "When the time is right for the both of you, it'll happen. Just know, you have a family around you for support, no matter what happens."

"Thanks, Mom." He looks down at Oliver and says, "Have you and Dad thought about adding to the family?"

I blanch. "Oh, no. Not gonna happen. Your sister is a handful, and I feel that once she graduates, your dad will suggest we move to California. I get the feeling he wants to be there and really focus on keeping the band relevant. Besides, I'm ready to be a grandma."

Noah laughs. "But is Liam Page ready to be a grandfather?"

Now it's my turn to chuckle. "I think there are days when yes he is. But then Betty Paige says something off the wall and scary, and he's reminded that he has a teenager at home."

"Scary?"

"Mostly about Mack and how much she loves him and so forth. She's been very vocal about her feelings, which I've encouraged. Your father squirms though. He remembers what he was like at Mack's age and doesn't want to think . . . well you don't need the details of your parents earlier years."

Noah smirks. "You're right."

Oliver starts to fuss, and I instantly get up, but Noah stands and starts walking around the room with him. It takes a few minutes, but Ollie quiets down and snuggles into Noah's neck. My son is a natural with Oliver and is going to make an amazing father someday.

NOAH, Oliver, and I spend the rest of the morning and into the afternoon sitting by the fire and playing board games. It's well after lunch when the front door opens, and multiple voices carry through the entryway. I get up and greet everyone and try to listen to what they have to say, but it's near impossible.

"I take it you had a good time," I say as Liam stops in front of me. He buries his cold face into the crook of my neck, making me squeal. I slap his chest and push him away. "You're freezing. Go sit by the fire."

Liam laughs and starts telling me about the ride, although I can't really keep up because multiple conversations are going on simultaneously.

"Where's Oliver?" Katelyn asks when she comes into the room. Her nose and cheeks are rosy red.

"He's sleeping," Noah tells her. I watch him as he moves toward Peyton. He reaches for her, not caring that she's an icicle, and pulls her into his arms. There's something about how they embrace, making me curious about whether Noah was truthful with me earlier. The way he's holding her, it's more like comfort. There is just something I can't shake.

Katelyn and Harrison disappear toward their room while Elle lingers in the kitchen. Mack, Paige, and Eden are talking about going night skiing. And Jenna and Jimmy announce they need to warm up in the pool.

"The pool sounds like an excellent idea. Want to go?" Liam asks.

"Yeah, sure," I say, but my eyes are still focused on Noah and Peyton.

"What are you doing?" Liam asks.

"What?" I look at him and shake my head.

"Whatever is going on, stop."

"Nothing is going on," I tell him, although I don't even believe the words coming out of my mouth. I hate that I'm looking for any sign of trouble with him. It's stupid, really. They're like Liam and me, or Katelyn and Mason—in love with each other most of their lives. Only with Noah and Peyton, they had to wait until it was socially acceptable to date. Not to mention legal. The more I watch them, the more I realize how much they remind me of Liam and me and they love we share. It's consuming. Almost like no one exists in our world. My parents hated it, as did his.

Liam drags me away from whatever scene I'm trying to develop in my mind and into our bedroom. He shuts the door and stalks toward me. I eye him with caution but also with desire. When he reaches me, his cold hands cup my face as his lips press against mine. "I missed you today," he says when we part.

"I missed you too." I tell him what Noah and I did all

day, and how relaxing it was, and how Oliver is such a good baby. Liam talks about their ride and how cold it was, but the diner was worth the trip.

"How was Mack?" I ask, still worried about him.

"You know, he's a good kid."

"Your daughter loves him."

He nods. "I know. They're us. I can see it in the way they look at each other. They gravitate toward one another. It's scary. I'm scared for them."

"We just have to make sure they know the consequences of their actions." I really can't stomach the idea of Betty Paige having sex right now or even next year, and I don't know what I'm going to do when or if she asks me how old I was when I lost my virginity—telling her to wait when I didn't would make me look like a hypocrite.

Liam sits down on the bed and pats the spot next to him. I happily sit there. "The last couple of nights, Mack and I have stayed up and talked some. He tells me about life at home. The fighting between his parents. And how he spends most of his time in his room with his headphones on. He doesn't want to move but also wants his mom and sister to stay in Beaumont. Mack's torn between his parents right now and feels lost. He thanked me for letting him stay with us and promised he would follow all my rules. I trust him, JoJo. I really do. But what has me worried is that he wants to go to college to play ball. Either football or baseball."

"That's good, right?"

Liam nods. "It is, but I think back to when I went through all of that and chose a school based on Mason, and how I chose to follow what my father wanted and not what I wanted. I remember how miserable I was and how much I hated school. Most of all, I remember the night I walked out on you, left you there in your dorm room, pregnant and alone. I don't want that for our daughter, and I'm not saying Mack will do that or Paige is going to end up pregnant at eighteen. All I'm saying is I see a lot of me in Mack, and it scares me."

"Why does that scare you, Liam? You're a good man. You didn't know I was pregnant. I know deep down, if you had, you would've stayed."

He smiles and kisses me. "I love you more than life, JoJo," he whispers against my lips.

"I love you too. Now tell me, why are you scared?"

Liam pulls away and looks into my eyes. "I want Paige to live life to the fullest. I want her to follow her dreams, not Mack's, or anything they create together. I want her to explore, travel, and find her passion before she settles down. I'm scared they're heading in our direction. When I was Mack's age, I cared about three things: football, Josie Preston, and having sex with her."

I can't help but blush even though the situation doesn't call for it. "We can't stop them from falling in love, but we can prepare them and encourage them to think for themselves. I think Mack has a good role model in Noah, and Paige does as well with the twins. And I think you overthink sometimes. We just gotta go with the flow, Mr. Page."

Liam growls and tackles me onto the bed. "You know, I brought my Santa hat. Tonight, you can sit on Santa's lap and tell him what you want for Christmas."

"Deal," I tell him. "But fair warning, I've been very, very naughty this year." I wink and get up before Liam can do anything. I'm to the door when I hear him groan into the blankets.

W hen you have a houseful of people, including three teenagers, and a brand-new baby, the Christmas tree is overflowing on Christmas morning. At some point, after everyone had arrived, Harrison, JD, and I decided that all three of us needed to play Santa. Handing out presents and wearing a Santa hat is something each of us does for our family, and it only made sense that we'd continue with our traditions. The only issue we couldn't decide was how it would work. Thankfully, we have brilliant women to guide us, men, along in our lives. I don't remember who blurted the solution out, but it made sense. The dads will take turns. It's as simple as that.

This Christmas is unlike any other, at least the ones we've had in the past. Everyone is here, except for a few people. We're missing Harrison's mom, Mason's dad, Ben, and Katelyn's parents. My mom, Josie's parents, and the Davises side of the family. But it's Mack who I'm focused on at the moment. I'm sure the boy feels awkward, celebrating such an important day without his family.

However, Josie has gone above and beyond to make sure he's comfortable. He has presents under the tree, mostly from Nick, who made sure his son wasn't going to go without gifts, but from us as well. Watching Mack move among our tight-knit family, it's like seeing what my future will be. He fits in, and that scares me. I think deep down I want him to be on edge and always on his best behavior. I think I want him to be like I was when I was his age, afraid of Mr. Preston. Although, that fear didn't stop me from being a complete shithead.

"Dad, are you going to stand there all morning?" Noah's voice brings me out of my reverie and to the present. He's sitting on the couch, with his wife and best friend curled into his side. Elle is sitting next to them. Nola's sitting on the last cushion, and Quinn is on the floor in front of his future wife. Katelyn and Harrison sit together on one of two love seats, with baby Oliver nestled in the middle. Jimmy and Jenna claimed the couch closest to the fireplace. Jenna's cold. Betty Paige, Eden, and Mack are on the floor, anxiously waiting for their presents. And my wife, the love of my life and the reason I am who I am, is patting the spot next to her. I push myself off the doorjamb and make my way toward her.

"Merry Christmas," I say as I sit down and kiss her just below her ear.

"Merry Christmas to you."

If I could meet and fall in love with her all over again, I would do it in a heartbeat. She's the best thing to ever happen to me, and I hate that I let her down for ten years of her life. I'll never stop trying to make up for what I put her through.

"Is it presents time?" Betty Paige asks. I have a feeling everyone is waiting, and not so patiently.

"JD, you're up first," Harrison says. JD stands and puts his Santa hat on. He tries to laugh like Santa while leaning back and holding his non-existent belly. The dude is skinny, always has been.

"I think you need to eat a sandwich, Santa," I blurt out. Everyone erupts with laughter, except for Jenna.

"He's perfect," she says.

"Thanks, wifey," JD replies. He crouches down and picks up the first package. It goes to Quinn. We thought about waiting for everyone to open their gift but realized we would be here forever, although that's not necessarily a bad thing. JD continues to pass out presents and then hands the Santa duties off to Harrison, who continues. By the time it's my turn, I'm down on all fours, under the tree, pulling out the last of the gifts.

Wrapping paper covers the floor, and boxes continue to stack on top of each other. Each of us has made a pile of our things along the wall to keep our space as clutter-free as possible. I come across a box with my name on it and do a double-take when I see who it's from. I glance at Mack, who's looking at the floor. I rip away the paper and open the box. Inside is a framed picture of Betty Paige and me. I'm crouched down and looking up at her, and her hand is on my cheek.

"Where did you get this?" I ask Mack.

"I took it," he says. "I didn't know how to thank you for . . ." he stops talking and takes a deep breath. "I thought you'd like it."

"I love it. Do you like photography?"

Mack nods. "I do."

"Do you have a camera?"

"Yes, it's not great, but it works. I'm saving to buy a new one."

I nod and turn my attention back to the picture. Candid shots like this mean more to me than the family posed photo. The image captures so much more. "This is amazing, Mack. Thank you." I stand and go to him. I hold my hand out, waiting for him to shake my hand, but when he sets his hand into mine, I pull him up instead and into my arms. "Truly an amazing gift. When we get back to Beaumont, remind me to show you some of the equipment I have, and we'll see what kind of pictures you can take."

"I'd like that, sir."

Mack and I have had a moment, one I never expected. When I let the boy go, I hand Josie's the frame. Tears form in her eyes almost instantly, but she wipes them away before anyone other than me can see them.

"I told you he'd love it," I hear Betty Paige say to Mack. She's right, I do.

With all the presents opened, and most of them put away, the wives head into the kitchen to start dinner, and the husbands clean. The kids got off easy, in my opinion, and head out to the slopes.

"Eden sure likes to snowboard," I say to JD.

"Yeah, she does, although I hope she doesn't give up surfing. This cold, wet shit ain't for me."

Harrison laughs. "You have it so easy." He slaps his hand down on JD's shoulder, who scoffs.

"You're an arse," he says to Harrison. "Bringing a baby home for Christmas. You have all the clocks going tick-tock, tick-tock."

"Not ours," I say. "JoJo and I are done having kids."

"Except now you have Mack," Harrison says.

I shake my head slowly. "Nick will be back by New Year's, and things will be back to normal. I'll go back to being the dad who loathes any boy who looks at my daughter."

"Except you like the kid," JD says. He's right, I do, and I'm not sure if that's a good thing or not.

After we have everything cleaned up, the men and Peyton head outside for a little game of football, and because Noah wants to play, he's the designated quarterback for both teams, and no one can tackle him. Except for maybe his wife. The last thing any of us want is for Noah to get hurt. He has to fly back to Portland tomorrow and get ready for his game next week. It's then that we'll celebrate Christmas with my mom. She'll happily miss the holidays, but she won't miss her grandson's football game.

Outside, we separate into teams. I take Peyton on mine because—well, why not. I've seen her play, and she could've undoubtedly started on the varsity at Beaumont High if she tried out for the team. There isn't a doubt in my mind that Mason would've let her if he was alive, and Nick felt the same way. He was prepared for her to show up in August of her freshman year. He already knew what position she'd play and everything. Honestly, I was a bit sad she didn't do it. I would've loved to cheer my ass off for her.

It's cold out but not as cold as it was earlier in the week. Noah crouches down, pretending he has a center in front of him. He looks at me, Quinn, and then Peyton calls the play and yells hike. Peyton and I take off running. We cross each other, with Harrison and JD hot on our heels, and leave Quinn available for the short pass. Elle is guarding her brother, but he's too tall and easily catches the pass from Noah. But Elle is sneaky fast and can grab her brother before he can get any farther.

"Second down," I yell as I run back.

"And short," Elle says, cocking her eyebrow at me. I put my arm around her, and we walk back to the line of scrimmage together.

"I knew you paid attention when we watched the games."

Elle winks and tosses the ball back to Noah. "I know more than you think, Uncle Liam."

"Lovely," I mutter.

Nola stands on our makeshift sideline, marking our imaginary downs and keeping time. We are only playing five-minute quarters due to the freezing air and elevation. I know that once we're inside, we're going to hack up a lung or two.

"Do you have room for one more?" I glance over at the voice to find Mack standing here.

"I thought you went skiing?"

"We did but came back."

"Where's Paige?" I ask.

Mack points to the house. "She's coming out to stand with Nola."

"All right, why don't you sub for Noah."

"Hey," Noah says, acting as if he's hurt. "What if Mack and I swap?"

"Yeah, whatever." I'm almost out of breath, and I think I've pulled a muscle.

Noah hands Mack the ball, and for a moment, they talk among themselves. "Traitor," I mumble at Noah, who just shakes his head. Mack takes up the center position, putting Peyton, Quinn, and me on defense.

"Let's go, Quinn. Hit someone."

I look over at Nola and then at Quinn. "She always into violence?"

He shakes his head and laughs. "Not normally. When we watch Noah's games, she cringes a lot."

"Me too," Peyton adds.

"Hey!" Noah yells from the sideline.

"Sorry, babe," his wife says back, although I'm not sure she means it.

Mack calls his play and points at me. *What the hell?* That's okay because I'm ready for him if he thinks he's going to run right past me. I get lower in my stance and wait for him to take his three steps back, only he doesn't. He takes five. Like I used to. Like Noah does. In this moment, I'm thankful there is snow on the ground, and none of Noah's receivers are here because I have a feeling Mack can throw the ball. I may not want to see what he can do here, but come football season, I'm going to have a front-row seat to his game.

He passes the ball off to Harrison, who runs right toward me, only when he gets close enough for me to grab, he tosses the ball behind to JD, who takes off running toward an empty field.

"Son of a bitch," I scream as JD enters the endzone, and of course, he dances in victory. "Smart play," I say to Mack. "Did your dad teach you to take five steps like that?"

He shakes his head. "No, sir."

"Where'd you learn it?"

"From watching old videos of you."

His words take the air from my lungs. Compared to my son, I was nothing of a quarterback. A high school kid dubbed the golden boy who flopped big time when he got to college. But Noah, he's the real deal and puts me to shame in the record books.

"I don't know what to say, Mack. I'm really honored."

Mack smiles and then ducks his head. Peyton, Noah, and Quinn come to me and start talking strategy, but I'm too focused on Mack. He approaches Harrison, Elle, and JD, and they huddle together. When Mack looks over his shoulder and smiles at me, I realize then that our relationship isn't going to be the typical father of the girl he's dating. It's going to be so much more.

Blow

Sexcation

HOLIDAY NOVELS

Santa's Secret

It's a Wonderful Holiday

THE DATING SERIES

A Date for Midnight

A Date with an Admirer

A Date for Good Luck

A Date for the Hunt

A Date for the Derby

A Date to Play Fore

A Date with a Foodie

A Date for the Fair

A Date for the Regatta

A Date for the Masquerade

A Date with a Turkey

A Date with an Elf

ABOUT HEIDI MCLAUGHLIN

Heidi McLaughlin is a New York Times, Wall Street Journal, and USA Today Bestselling author of The Beaumont Series, The Boys of Summer, and The Archers.

Originally, from the Pacific Northwest, she now lives in picturesque Vermont, with her husband, two daughters, and their three dogs.

In 2012, Heidi turned her passion for reading into a full-fledged literary career, writing over twenty novels, including the acclaimed Forever My Girl.

Heidi's first novel, Forever My Girl, has been adapted into a motion picture with LD Entertainment and Roadside Attractions, starring Alex Roe and Jessica Rothe, and opened in theaters on January 19, 2018.

Don't miss more books by Heidi McLaughlin! Sign up for her newsletter, or join the fun in her fan group!

Connect with Heidi!
www.heidimclaughlin.com

Made in the USA
Middletown, DE
07 June 2021